EXTRAORDINARY

RENDITION

A Special Agent Dylan Kane Thriller

Also by J. Robert Kennedy

James Acton Thrillers

The Protocol	*Amazon Burning*	*Wrath of the Gods*
Brass Monkey	*The Riddle*	*The Templar's Revenge*
Broken Dove	*Blood Relics*	*The Nazi's Engineer*
The Templar's Relic	*Sins of the Titanic*	*Atlantis Lost*
Flags of Sin	*Saint Peter's Soldiers*	*The Cylon Curse*
The Arab Fall	*The Thirteenth Legion*	*The Viking Deception*
The Circle of Eight	*Raging Sun*	*Keepers of the Lost Ark*
The Venice Code	*Wages of Sin*	*The Tomb of Genghis Khan*
Pompeii's Ghosts		*The Manila Deception*

Special Agent Dylan Kane Thrillers

Rogue Operator	*Death to America*	*Retribution*
Containment Failure	*Black Widow*	*State Sanctioned*
Cold Warriors	*The Agenda*	*Extraordinary Rendition*

Templar Detective Thrillers

The Templar Detective	*The Sergeant's Secret*	*The Code Breaker*
The Parisian Adulteress	*The Unholy Exorcist*	

Kriminalinspektor Wolfgang Vogel Mysteries
The Colonel's Wife

Delta Force Unleashed Thrillers

Payback	*The Lazarus Moment*	*Forgotten*
Infidels	*Kill Chain*	

Detective Shakespeare Mysteries

Depraved Difference	*Tick Tock*	*The Redeemer*

Zander Varga, Vampire Detective
The Turned

EXTRAORDINARY RENDITION

A Special Agent Dylan Kane Thriller

J. ROBERT KENNEDY

ISBN: 9781990418518

First Edition

10 9 8 7 6 5 4 3 2 1

For Michèle Easey, who helped rekindle it all.

EXTRAORDINARY RENDITION

RENDITION

A Special Agent Dylan Kane Thriller

"Any organization or citizen shall support, assist and cooperate with the state intelligence work in accordance with the law, and keep the secrets of the national intelligence work known to the public."

Article 7, Chinese National Intelligence Law
Passed June 27, 2017

"There is no force that can shake the foundation of this great nation. No force can stop the Chinese people and the Chinese nation forging ahead."

Chinese President Xi Jinping
October 1, 2019

PREFACE

One day, during the presidency of George H. W. Bush, he received a standard morning intelligence briefing. This particular meeting included the national security advisor Brent Scowcroft, and the CIA director Robert Gates, as well as one other participant unfamiliar to the President—something not unusual, as many one-off attendees were often invited to give a specific briefing.

This individual gave a talk regarding the latest technologies employed by the CIA to disguise their agents. At the end of her briefing, she indicated she would now remove one of these new technologies. The President, the former head of the CIA, stopped her. He wanted to try and figure it out himself. He rose and circled her, but was unable to determine what form of disguise she was using.

The moment he returned to his desk, she peeled off her face, revealing her true self hidden behind a mask so realistic, even the former head of the Central Intelligence Agency couldn't tell. The reveal shocked everyone in the room, and photos of that meeting were only recently declassified.

The extremely sophisticated and realistic face mask was her and her team's brainchild, and has been employed by the CIA for decades.

And who was this mystery woman? The CIA's Disguise Chief, Jonna Mendez, a titan in the intelligence world.

This technology, along with all of the technologies described in this book, are real, and are in use today by various governments around the world.

Falls Church, Virginia

Lee Fang loved the high an intense workout afforded her, though sometimes a leisurely jog through her new hometown was as enjoyable in other ways. After all, an all-out sprint down the streets of Falls Church would draw attention, and would likely end up in several collisions.

She was as fit as any athlete, professional or otherwise, and liked to keep it that way. It was a holdover from her former life—Chinese Special Forces, a major in the Beijing Military Region Special Forces Unit.

She had loved her job, the intensity of it, the adrenaline, the sense of accomplishment.

The violence.

She was small compared to a man, especially the Americans she was now surrounded by. But technique easily made up for that. She was strong for a woman, a turn of phrase that had her bristling at times, though biology had to be acknowledged. Not all men were stronger than all women, though that wasn't the most important thing. A man might

3

deliver the strongest blow, but if that blow was dodged and his kneecap taken out a moment later, he was down, no matter how strong he was.

Or she could just put two in his chest from a distance.

I miss that life.

It wasn't the killing. She never enjoyed that, but she would do it when necessary. It was the act of *doing* something. She had been forced to betray her country a few years ago, an act she didn't regret. What the rogue generals were doing was wrong, and hadn't been approved by the Party. She had defended herself, killing one of them, then delivered her precious intel to the Americans in an attempt to head off a coup in Washington, aided by her own military leadership.

The crisis had been averted, the day saved, but her life as she knew it was over.

She was a traitor to her country, relegated to a life of exile in a grateful America, where she was paid a generous pension and forbidden from working in any job related to her field.

I can't even be a cook because it involves knives.

She didn't regret her decision. It was the right thing to do despite the cost.

And because of it, she had met the love of her life.

Dylan Kane.

She had never thought she'd fall in love with an American. Caucasian men had never been her thing, though her exposure to them in China was only through television and the movies, both mediums of which she had little time for back then.

Her job had been her life.

Dylan Kane had been the CIA asset assigned to extract her from China, and once saved, they had discovered a shared pain that drew them together.

Loneliness.

What had begun as a friendship quickly blossomed into a romance, then a love so intense, she would never return to China even if afforded the opportunity.

Her life was here now, with the man she intended to spend the rest of her days with.

She rounded a corner, spotting a van out of the corner of her eye making the same turn but not accelerating out of it. Her trouble-radar had a shot of adrenaline heightening her senses and she slowed slightly.

"I got me a case of Yellow Fever, baby! Can you help me out?"

Fang came to an abrupt halt and stepped into a coffee shop as the teenagers roared away laughing. It was something that happened to her all the time, though it was the first since she had moved from Philadelphia. The smaller town of Falls Church was far more civilized. In Philly, she had taken to wearing baggy clothing to hide her body, and it was something that pissed her off. Why should she have to hide how she looked because some men couldn't control themselves?

And unlike back home, I can't beat the living shit out of them.

She smiled slightly. She could, but…

"Men are pigs."

She turned to see a woman sipping her coffee. "Excuse me?"

"What just happened. They're pigs."

"Not all of them."

5

"You found yourself a good one?"

She smiled as she pushed open the door to leave. "The best."

"Then you hold on to him, honey, they're few and far between!"

Fang resumed her jog, putting a little speed on, returning to the sanctuary of her apartment she shared with Kane. She spotted her new home and relaxed, not realizing how tense she was from the ridiculous encounter.

Her life was always one lived on the razor's edge. She had to always be watching out for the unusual, for anything that might be a threat. And in the entire time she had lived in America, not once had anything happened.

When will you let it go? Eventually, you have to acknowledge they're not coming for you.

She entered her apartment building and headed for the elevator, smiling at the caretaker as he swept the lobby. "Hi Titanic, how are you today?"

The middle-aged man stopped and leaned on his broom. "I'm still on the right side of the dirt, so I guess life is good. How about you, Miss Lee?"

She laughed. "I can't complain."

"Cuz' no one will listen, right?"

She stepped onto the elevator as the doors opened. "Dylan listens, though sometimes he pretends not to."

"You have yourself a nice day, Miss Lee."

"You too!" she replied through the closing doors. Bob "Titanic" McCormick always made her feel good. He reminded her of the handyman at her apartment back in Beijing where she had grown up. Friendly, helpful, and always repeating the same jokes.

It made her feel warm inside.

She inserted the key to her apartment into the lock and turned it, opening the door.

And immediately a taser was shoved into her stomach. The electricity flowed, but the protective undergarment she wore just for such an occasion—provided by her apparently justified paranoid boyfriend—absorbed and spread the electricity over a greater area, reducing though not eliminating its effect.

She snapped out a kick, her foot catching her attacker in the jewels as two more emerged from behind the door.

Then another three.

All Chinese.

They finally came for you.

That meant this was to the death.

She shifted to the right, toward the smallest of her assailants as the first writhed on the ground in agony. She redirected his blow then swept his feet, grabbing his arm on his way down then planting her foot at his armpit, twisting the arm out of its socket. A hand grabbed her from behind and she dropped, using her body weight to break the still unestablished hold, then jerked her elbow up and into his scrotum, the remaining three backing away as they finally drew their weapons.

They meant to take her alive.

That much was obvious, though it still meant death at the other end of this journey. She would be interrogated and tortured for weeks if not months or years, then finally put to death for treason.

She'd rather die here, now, and get it over with.

She grabbed one of her victims around the neck, putting him in a chokehold as she backed toward the door. "Come any closer, he dies."

Her warning was delivered in Chinese—there was no use wasting time with pretenses.

All three advanced.

She snapped her man's neck and shoved him toward the men as she kicked her first assailant in the head, then dropped her foot down hard on his neck, snapping it.

She faced four, unarmed, and now that they were aware of her capabilities, she didn't expect the rest to go down so easily.

This was about to be over, even if their orders were to take her alive.

No more would be willing to die for the sake of following orders.

They advanced, splitting apart as she backed toward the now closed door, cursing the pneumatic closer. She could yell for help, but that might get one of her innocent neighbors killed.

And Kane was on a mission somewhere in the world, too far to help her.

She took a fighting stance. "Let's do this, bitches."

Leroux/White Residence, Fairfax Towers

Falls Church, Virginia

"That's not like her."

"Context, hon."

Sherrie White glanced up from her phone at her boyfriend, Chris Leroux. "Oh, I texted Fang to see if she was ready to go to lunch, but she didn't reply."

"Maybe she's in the shower. Weren't you two supposed to go for a jog together first?"

"Yeah, but I tweaked my ankle during training yesterday. I have to take it easy for a few days before I can recertify for active duty."

Leroux gave her a peck on the cheek. "My girlfriend, the super-agent."

She grabbed him by the back of the neck. "Is that all you've got for me?"

He eyed her. "I thought you had lunch plans."

"I do, but I can have a proper kiss, can't I?"

He smiled and planted one on her that had her tingling from the inside out.

She sighed. "You're getting damned good at that."

He winked. "Practice makes perfect."

She pouted. "Who are you practicing on when I'm not around?"

He wagged a finger. "A CIA man never tells." He opened the door. "See you tonight. Love you."

She blew him a kiss. "Love you too."

The door closed and she leaned back on the couch, hugging herself. Life was good. So good. She had just been promoted, she lived with the man she loved, she had a few good friends—all she had ever needed—and had no complaints. Her childhood had sucked with her parents being killed in a car accident when she was a teenager, but life had improved slowly, then dramatically once she met Leroux.

She chuckled as she pictured how awkward he used to be. He still was to a point, and was definitely a geek compared to her, but she loved every single little quirk.

But he was a man now, and gawd could he satisfy her—once she had taught him a few tricks.

She pushed to her feet, deciding waiting for Fang to reply was pointless when she lived in the same building. She put on her jacket then paused. It *was* unlike Fang not to respond.

Better safe than sorry.

She headed to the bedroom and retrieved her weapon from the gun locker. She removed her jacket and put on her shoulder holster, slipping her Glock inside along with her suppressor in its special slot. She didn't bother with extra ammo. She was certain nothing was amiss, it was simply an overabundance of caution and years of training at the CIA that had her worried.

Maybe you're overreacting.

She stared at herself in the mirror.

Go get her, then come back here and put the weapon back.

She nodded then closed the locker, minutes later approaching the apartment her best friend Fang shared with Leroux's best friend Kane.

And paused.

She was certain she had heard something. A grunt or a groan.

Something.

She smiled slightly.

Maybe Dylan got home early and they're bumpin' uglies.

She pulled a small magnetic device off her keychain, designed to mimic a mini-flashlight. She pressed it against the peephole then pulled out her phone, launching the app, the image the device would capture certain to be titillating.

Her eyes bulged as she suppressed a gasp. Two men had Fang at gunpoint, her friend badly beaten and lying on the floor, her hands tied behind her back. Whatever had happened had just finished, and Fang had lost.

For now.

Sherrie drew her weapon and screwed the suppressor in place, not willing to fire without it and have neighbors not only poke their heads out their doors like idiots, but also not willing to blow their covers unnecessarily. She took aim with her right arm extended in front of her, the phone in her left hand, then adjusted her trajectory.

She squeezed the trigger twice then adjusted right, firing twice more. Her first target went down in a heap, but the second managed to only get himself winged. She fired four into the wood surrounding the lock, weakening the structure, then kicked the door open as she surged inside, regretting the choice to not bring extra ammo. She swung her weapon toward the second man and fired twice as he dropped behind the couch, evidently missing if his continued efforts to scramble away were any indication.

Suddenly a plastic bag was dropped over her head from behind. She immediately elbowed him in the stomach, but his grip was like iron. She reached up to poke a finger through the plastic so she could breathe when a fourth man rushed from another room, grabbing her arms as she gasped for breath, her already pounding heart chewing rapidly through her oxygen. Someone tased her and she fell to her knees, her breaths shallow now, her gasps growing less frequent as her world went dark.

She was going to die.

And her only thought was of how her beloved would once again regress into his shell, and be alone for the rest of his life.

I'm so sorry!

Lobby, Fairfax Towers
Falls Church, Virginia

CIA Analyst Supervisor Chris Leroux stepped out of the elevator, already late for work. In his haste, he almost ran headlong into a maintenance crew, pulling up just in time.

"Sorry guys, my bad."

None of the four men replied and he chalked it up to a possible language barrier, all four Asian, all with haircuts that would appear more at home on the other side of the Pacific, suggesting they were new to the country.

He jogged the rest of the way to his car and started up the engine, firing a quick text to Sherrie.

Did you find Fang?

He put on his seatbelt, pulled up Tommy Granger's latest podcast, something he was enjoying immensely, then frowned at the lack of a reply from Sherrie.

They must be gabbing.

13

He pulled out of his parking spot then headed toward the office, thinking about Sherrie and Fang. He had no idea what women did alone with each other. Were they like guys? He grunted. He didn't know what guys were like. He had been the king of the dorks in high school, friendless until the popular jock Dylan Kane needed tutoring. They had become friends, and Kane his protector, though beyond him, he had been alone.

His Friday night was sitting in front of the television, sharing a pizza with his parents.

It had been pathetic.

Life hadn't improved. In fact, after he was recruited by the CIA and moved closer to work, he had been painfully alone, not even his parents there to keep him company. He simply threw himself into his work, then was delighted to discover his best and only friend, whom he had lost touch with after high school, worked at the CIA as well. Though with Kane operational, he was rarely in country, but when he was, they would always get together.

It was Leroux's hard work and talent that had drawn the attention of his boss, National Clandestine Service Chief for the CIA Leif Morrison, who, before bringing him into the inner circle, had tested his loyalty with a honey pot—Sherrie White, who was assigned to seduce him then pump him for information.

He had passed the test, but was devastated to learn the woman he was falling in love with had been playing him.

Or so he had thought. It turned out she had fallen for her target and had begged to be reassigned. Unfortunately, timing was critical, and the request had been denied. It had been his best friend who had reunited them, and they had been together ever since.

And life was better than it had ever been.

In fact, for the first time, he was truly happy. He had even become used to being the boss, his promotion giving him a team of almost a dozen, a team that he had gained the respect of by constantly proving he deserved the job, despite his young age.

He spotted the gates for CIA Headquarters ahead and sighed.

I love my life.

Then frowned as he paused his podcast, his text message to Sherrie still unanswered.

What the hell are those two doing?

Fairfax Towers

Falls Church, Virginia

CIA Special Agent Dylan Kane leaned against the back of the elevator, his eyes closed, his entire body exhausted from his latest mission—not every assignment meant a five-star hotel to relax in. In the past, he'd head off to some resort in Thailand or such, drink himself into a stupor, and enjoy the company of the local ladies.

But that was behind him. He had forgiven himself for what he had been a part of years ago, accepting that the innocent deaths weren't his fault, and that there was nothing he could have done to avert the missile strike that took the lives of so many whose only guilt was that by association.

And he had found himself an honest woman.

Lee Fang had changed his life. They had changed each other's lives. He had extracted her from China to the safety of the United States, and she had extracted him from the death spiral that had been his life.

Now he had something to live for.

At first, he had been concerned it would affect his job. One of his assets was the fact he had never cared if he died. He preferred to work alone, had no friends, and little contact with his family, though it wasn't an estranged relationship anymore, things improving dramatically since his father discovered he hadn't left the US Army to be a glorified insurance salesman.

With the family relationship repaired, Fang giving him a reason to come home, and Leroux and his partner Sherrie giving him the outlets he needed to get things off his chest, his life was complete. The lies were finished. His circle was made up of people who knew who he really was, knew what he did, and often were involved at some level. He could share his troubles and frustrations, and it had allowed him to work out issues that had haunted him for years.

He exited the elevator, glancing at his phone, his texts to Fang still unanswered.

And it had him concerned.

Fang was rarely away from her phone, and it had been almost an hour since his first text to her.

She could be out for a run.

There were any number of reasons she might not be answering, though his vocation had him always fearing the worst.

He reached toward the door with his key then paused. The door seemed different. He reached forward and pressed a finger against it then pulled it away, finding paint on the tip.

Huh. I didn't think it needed to be painted.

He inserted the key and opened the door, stepping inside. "Hey, babe, I'm home!"

There was no answer.

Must be out.

He started for the bedroom to change when he paused. The couch was out of place. Only slightly, maybe a few inches, and the throw cushions had all been piled on it instead of spread about the other chairs in the room. He slowly turned his head, his trained eyes examining every detail. The room was as he had left it two weeks ago, and was meticulously neat as Fang always kept it.

Yet something was wrong.

Too many things appeared just slightly out of place.

His heart hammered.

As if someone who didn't know exactly where things should go had straightened up.

He quickly searched the rest of the apartment, making certain she wasn't there, then returned to the living area, suddenly spotting what was throwing him off the entire time.

A large blanket was lying over the back of the couch.

A blanket he didn't recognize, and was definitely not Fang's taste. This had a Mexican flare to it, beautiful bright colors and patterns. Fang preferred solid colors, no patterns, trending toward harsh reds or solid blacks.

She would never buy that.

He stepped to the side of the couch, getting a better angle on what the blanket might be hiding, and controlled his reaction as he spotted what appeared to be a hole in the back.

"Maybe Chris and Sherrie know where she went."

He headed out the door, locking it behind him, before going down the elevator and climbing into his car, hoping the eyes and ears he now feared littered his apartment bought his ruse.

For every fiber of his being was telling him something was wrong.

He dialed Leroux as he pulled out of the parking lot, praying he was mistaken.

Operations Center 2, CIA Headquarters

Langley, Virginia

"She's supposed to be at lunch with Sherrie. Why?"

"When's the last time you heard from either of them?"

Leroux's stomach churned at the concern in Kane's voice. "I saw Sherrie maybe an hour ago at the apartment. She wasn't able to reach Fang about their lunch date, so she went to see her after I left for work. I texted her but never heard back. I assumed they were too busy chatting and weren't paying attention to their phones." He pulled his out. "Let me try again." He fired off a quick text.

911. Respond immediately.

"Anything?"

Leroux frowned, sweat beading on his upper lip. "No." He turned to Randy Child, his team's wunderkind when it came to computers. "Track Agent White and Lee Fang's phones."

"On it." Child worked his keyboard then indicated the large displays that curved across the entire front of the operations center. "They're both offline. Last active ping for both of them looks like your apartment building."

"When?"

"Fang's about an hour ago, Sherrie's about ten minutes later."

Leroux drew a deep breath, steadying his nerves. "Dylan, I've got a bad feeling about this. It's not like them to turn off their phones. Not in our business."

"Me too. Get me something to work with."

"Will do. I'll let the Chief know one of his agents is missing."

"Do that. And send a crew to sweep the apartment. If they left any listening devices behind, I can't be the one who discovers them. I'm just a lowly insurance investigator."

"We're on it."

Unknown Location

Fang jolted awake, panic momentarily setting in at the unfamiliar surroundings. It was completely dark, her entire body ached from the fight she had been in, and ultimately lost, six trained men against one trained woman, no matter how good, still odds even Kane would have had difficulty with.

But her pounding head dominated her suffering at the moment.

She had been injected with something, a lucky jab from behind that had proven enough to take her out of the fight.

Sherrie!

She remembered her friend entering the apartment, gunfire, and little else beyond glimpses through her drugged haze of a beating savage in its ferocity.

I hope she's okay.

Yet she knew her friend wasn't.

She couldn't have been.

Fang struggled against her bonds, her shoulders tight against whatever space confined her. She was lying on her back, and could hear what sounded like an engine running, a vibration pulsing through her body.

She was in a vehicle. Perhaps a truck of some sort. She had no idea how long she had been out. It could be minutes or days, but the fact her bladder wasn't troubling her, and she didn't feel as if she had soiled herself, she guessed less than a couple of hours.

Long enough for her to be far away from her apartment.

She had only one last move to play.

"Help!" she shouted, her gag muffling her plea.

Somebody pounded on the box she was confined in—for she was certain that's what it was. "Speak Chinese from now on! Your days of speaking English are behind you!"

Her skin went cold as a rush of anxiety swept over her, confirming her worst fears.

For the warning had been delivered in Mandarin.

They had indeed found her.

And her life was over.

Director Morrison's Office, CIA Headquarters
Langley, Virginia

"And you're sure they didn't just turn off their phones for a girl's night out?"

Leroux shook his head, dismissing his boss' suggestion, though he would have asked himself if he were in Director Morrison's position. "No, sir. First, it's lunchtime, and I've never known them to do anything wild at this hour, and with who and what they are, there's no way they would turn off their phones."

Morrison agreed. "Pull whatever resources you need. Find my agent."

"And Lee Fang?"

"I'm guessing if you find Agent White, you'll find her."

Leroux chewed his cheek for a moment as he processed the situation. "We can't really put out a missing person's report on her. It'll blow Sherrie's cover for any future ops."

Morrison leaned back in his chair. "Then what do you propose?"

"We'll pull footage, see if we can find a lead, then put out a BOLO on the vehicle or whoever we find is connected."

"You're forgetting one thing."

Leroux's eyes narrowed. "What?"

"Who Fang is."

"I'm not sure I follow you."

"That's because you're too close to this. You're focusing on your girlfriend, not the situation." Morrison leaned forward, placing his elbows on his desk. "Who was taken first?"

"I'm not sure. I guess Fang, since she was late meeting Sherrie."

"Exactly. Fang is a nobody to everyone except the Chinese."

"Maybe it's some other type of crime. Rape. Abduction."

"Do you really think that a single person could take out both Fang and Sherrie? Two highly trained operatives?"

Leroux frowned, his boss right. "I would hope not."

"Which means more than one was involved, which means a conspiracy, and it's definitely Fang from what you've told me."

"But why fix up the apartment like Dylan described?"

"Because they wanted to delay things. Only Dylan would notice the difference, but they don't know who he is. Every minute they buy, is a minute they have to put some distance between them and the crime scene. That means this was well-planned. They had a team waiting for her, then another to do the clean-up."

A wave of weakness swept over Leroux. "Oh my God!"

"What?"

"I saw them!"

"Who?"

"The clean-up crew. Four men came onto the elevator just as I got off. All Asian."

"Did you see their faces?"

Leroux nodded.

"Then that means the cameras did too."

"I'll get the footage, but it almost confirms it was the Chinese."

"Agreed. The question is, what is their end game? It has to be her past."

"So this is an extraordinary rendition situation."

"What else could it be? They've been looking for her since we gave her asylum. They find her, take her back, put her on trial, execute her."

Leroux went cold. "Which means Sherrie was never part of their plan." He paled. "She's dead, isn't she?"

Morrison shook his head, his jaw squaring. "No one is dead until I see a body."

Unknown Location

Sherrie groaned as the fog of pain slowly lifted enough for her to become aware she had no idea where she was. She moved her limbs to find herself bound at the wrists and ankles, and her aching jaw made it painfully obvious she had been gagged for some time.

She winced as she drew a breath, then gasped at the pain. Several ribs were cracked or worse, and her breathing was labored. Her head pounded, and from the intensity of it, she was quite certain a steel-toed boot had kicked her in the back of the head.

Concussion.

She had been beaten mercilessly, kicked by two of the men, no doubt pissed she had crashed their little party and killed one of their own.

But she was alive.

The question was for how long?

She struggled to move in the confined space, an overwhelming stench the only thing that gave her any sense of her surroundings, but that was nothing to go on.

She sat up, or at least attempted to, then cried out as her ribs revealed they were broken. An overwhelming headache blinded her and she fell back, her world black.

McDonald's

Arlington Blvd, Falls Church, Virginia

Kane swallowed another bite of his sausage and egg McMuffin then took a swig from his large Diet Coke. McDonald's breakfasts were one of his true vices, rarely exercised unless in country. And now that they were an all-day affair, he could enjoy them at any hour.

Though today he was just going through the motions. He was consumed by the disappearance of Fang, and of course Sherrie, yet there was nothing he could do but wait. Leroux's team would find something. They always did. And the moment the sweep team cleared his apartment, he'd return to properly gear up, his emergency kit in the false bottom of his trunk inadequate for what he suspected might be ahead.

A text arrived on his Apple Car Play display from Leroux indicating the all-clear for his return. He hoovered the rest of his food then put his seatbelt on and fired up the engine. As he put the car in gear, he dialed Leroux.

"What did they find?"

"Eyes and ears in every room, just like you suspected."

Kane cursed. "Any idea how long they've been there?"

"Assuming Fang does a standard sweep every day like you said, our guys said she would have caught them, so any time after she did her last sweep. I'm guessing they were planted this morning, either while she was out, or after she got back."

Kane turned onto the road. "She was out?"

"Yeah, she went for a run. Sherrie was supposed to go with her, but tweaked her ankle yesterday during training."

"Any idea whose work it is?"

"Our guys say it looks Chinese."

Kane growled. "Why am I not surprised? Okay, I'll be at the apartment in a few minutes. Have you found anything yet?"

"No. We're pulling footage now, but so far nothing. Can you get the building security footage? It isn't networked, so we don't have access to it, and I think I might have seen the cleaners in the elevator."

Kane's eyes widened. "You're kidding me! Would you recognize them?"

"I doubt it. They were getting on the elevator as I was getting off. I only saw them for a few seconds."

"What do you remember?"

"They were all similar. Asian, dark hair, bad haircuts, slim."

"So, not very helpful."

"I'm afraid not. If we get that footage, though, we might be able to identify them."

"It'll be my first stop."

Unknown Location

Fang had no doubt she was in a truck or something similar, the stops and starts, along with the turns, indicating they were still underway. To where, she had no idea. Nobody on the other side of what she had begun to think of as her coffin, had said anything since her warning to speak Chinese.

The vehicle came to a halt and the engine shut off.

Wherever they had been heading, they were there. An airplane roared overhead, and the distinct odor of jet fuel filled her nostrils. They were at the airport, and as soon as she was on an airplane, her fate was sealed.

She kicked out with her feet, hitting the bottom of her coffin, and slammed her shoulders from side to side as she yelled into her gag, hoping someone might hear her.

But there was no reaction from her captors, just a hissing sound then a foul odor as she slowly lost consciousness.

There'd be no escape for her today.

Operations Center 2, CIA Headquarters
Langley, Virginia

Leroux stared at the camera feeds showing his apartment building from various angles. "I saw a cleaning crew getting on the elevator. See if you can find any vehicles near there that might fit the description."

Randy Child tapped a few keys then spun in his chair, finishing with an arm pointed toward an enlarged feed. "I can do better than that."

Leroux tilted his head at the unusual angle. "What am I looking at?"

"One of your neighbors has a camera set up on his balcony. I think he likes people-watching. It's aimed at the parking lot."

Sonya Tong, one of Leroux's senior analysts and his number two, grunted. "More likely he or she doesn't trust their spouse."

Child shrugged. "Maybe, but whoever it is, doesn't understand security. They've just left the default password on the device. I'm about to get into their cloud storage...and I'm in."

Leroux stepped closer to the display. "Back it up to when I texted Sherrie." He checked his phone. "11:35. Go back about ten minutes before that."

Child worked his station and the footage started to play from the requested timecode.

"Speed it up."

Child complied, the footage racing through when Leroux held up a finger. "There. Slow it down."

Child tapped his keyboard and they all watched as a white box van parked, the four Asian men he had seen earlier climbing out. They headed into the building, where they didn't have coverage yet.

"Okay, run it forward, let's see when they come out."

Less than thirty minutes later, they reappeared, three large bags over their shoulders.

Body bags?

Bile filled Leroux's mouth as Child echoed his thoughts.

"Holy shit! You don't think—"

Leroux remembered the Chief's words. "Unless I see their bodies, neither of them is dead. Understood?"

Child's head dipped. "Yes, sorry."

Leroux turned to face his young underling. "Don't worry about it. Zoom in." The image expanded. "I think there's little doubt those are bodies. See if you can pull a height from those bags. Head to toe."

Child manipulated the image, lines displaying on the screen as he mapped the bulges in the bag to body parts, then smiled. "Good news! Best guess is they're all over five-eight."

Leroux sighed, his shoulders slumping with relief. "They have at least a few inches on both of them."

Tong shook her head in admiration. "That means they managed to kill three of their attackers."

Leroux took some satisfaction in the knowledge, though the fact might make the survivors less likely to let their hostages live. "I have a feeling they weren't expecting that, otherwise they would have had a dolly or something to take the bodies out with." He slapped his hands together. "Okay, Sonya, I want your team to start tracking that van forward and back. I want to know where it went and where it came from."

Tong nodded. "On it."

"Randy, roll back that footage. I want to see who else goes in and out. This was the clean-up crew, not the primary team."

Child returned to the arrival of the van, then rolled it back from there. Leroux watched as neighbors he'd seen for years came and went, then pointed. "Stop. Run it normal speed."

They watched a cargo van roll up and two Asian men get out, heading into the building. A couple of minutes later, a car arrived with two more Asian men, then a third vehicle with another two.

"That's six men for just Fang?" Child whistled. "Is she that good?"

Leroux nodded. "She is. Fast-forward. Let's see what we see."

Child pointed at the same time as Leroux. "There's Fang."

"Back from her run." About five minutes later one of the men left the building and retrieved two large, empty duffel bags from the back of the van. He returned inside, then a few minutes later three men left, the duffel bags bulging. One was placed in the back of the van, the other in the trunk of the second vehicle to arrive. Each of the men then drove one of the vehicles out of frame.

"Sonya, have your team track those as well."

"On it."

Child spun in his chair. "They took Sherrie and Fang, but left the bodies of their buddies? That's cold."

Leroux returned to his station. "The mission was to capture Fang."

"Dead or alive?"

"Alive, otherwise this would have been a lot easier. They would have just shot her then left her body." He shook his head. "No, they wanted her alive."

"And Sherrie?"

Leroux tensed. "Wrong place, wrong time."

"But she's alive, right?"

Leroux blew a burst of air through his lips. "I...don't know. They cleaned the apartment, which means they didn't want anyone to know what had happened for as long as possible. They couldn't leave her there, so they might have taken her body."

Tong shook her head. "You're forgetting one thing, boss."

"What's that?"

"They left three bodies there already. Why not four? Why would they bother taking her if she were dead? The only reason to take her is if she's still alive. They couldn't risk her raising the alarm."

Leroux brightened, sitting upright in his chair. "You're right! But why take her? Why not just kill her?"

Tong shrugged. "Would you kill a CIA agent on American soil?"

Child's eyes narrowed. "How would they know she's an agent?"

"Probably the way she fought. Maybe her weapon. If there were three dead there, then that probably means shots were fired. And that means a suppressor, otherwise the police would have been called. No law-abiding citizen goes around with one of those."

"Does Sherrie?" asked Child.

Leroux nodded. "Yes, her holster is designed to hold it."

"Would Fang?"

He shook his head. "No. Knowing her and Dylan, I'm sure there's one in the apartment, if not ten, but she would have been jumped the moment she entered, and she wouldn't dare carry a weapon on the street in case she got stopped by the police. Too many questions."

Tong agreed. "So, if a suppressor-equipped weapon was used, it was used by Sherrie, and because of that, they knew she had to be some sort of operative. Their orders didn't include how to handle that eventuality, so they subdued her and took her with Fang while waiting for orders on how to deal with her."

Leroux exhaled loudly. "It's as good a theory as any."

Child frowned. "Yeah, but what did those orders eventually turn out to be?"

Over Arlington, Virginia

Special Agent Brooklyn Tanner, leader of Echo Team, a CIA unit seconded to Homeland Security so they could operate legally on US soil, stared at the streets below from their chopper. One of their own had been kidnapped, or worse, yet local law enforcement couldn't be involved.

Not yet.

And that meant time was of the essence.

Control had told her almost nothing about the initial target, which meant it was highly classified, and despite her clearance level, that still meant need to know.

And she apparently didn't.

"We're almost there," said the pilot over the headset.

"Copy that."

Her team checked their gear as the pilot descended. Two cars and a van had arrived at the victim's location first. The two cars had been tracked to a local Walmart parking lot. According to Control, one of the victims had been put in the trunk of one of the vehicles, but the cars were parked in a dead zone with no camera coverage, so they had no idea if they were still there.

It was as if the vehicle dumping point had been picked purposefully, which meant these people had access to intel they shouldn't.

And that likely meant foreign government.

Her mind raced with possibilities. Russians? Chinese? North Koreans? Iranians? There were a lot of options, and for the moment, she had no intel to suggest any or none.

Though she might be about to find out.

"Mask up!"

Her team pulled up their facemasks to protect their identities, as what they were about to do was very public. She peered out the window and spotted the cars, still parked in the dead zone. "There they are! Secure the area, then check the cars. They might be boobytrapped!"

Unknown Location

Sherrie jolted awake, the sudden movement sending a wave of pain and nausea sweeping through her as her head and ribs screamed in agony.

Yet something had woken her.

Something loud.

It was overwhelming, her entire body vibrating with the sound, yet in her delirium she had no clue what it might be. Vomit erupted and she jerked her head to the side, the effort intensely painful, enough for her to recognize her concussion was growing worse.

She had to stay awake.

Though she was already fading, the sound that had woken her lost to the fog of her suffering. The world spun, the blackness of her prison deepened by the darkness of her mind losing the battle to remain conscious.

Walmart Supercenter, Kings Crossing

Arlington, Virginia

The chopper hit the ground with a bounce, but that didn't stop Tanner and her team from surging through the open doors, fanning out as their ride lifted off to provide eyes in the sky if needed. Four of her team took the corners as customers scattered, terrified at what they were witnessing.

And she didn't blame them.

The new assault team uniforms now worn by SWAT and other similar units were like something out of a dystopian science fiction movie a decade or two ago.

But we do look cool.

Two of her team swept both cars with RF scanners then searched for boobytraps without touching the vehicles. Her second, Michael Lyons, gave a thumbs up.

"I think we're clear."

"You think?"

He shrugged. "Hey, wouldn't be the first time we were wrong."

She stepped closer. Both cars were empty, but their victim was supposed to be in one of the trunks. "This is Homeland Security! Is anyone in the car?"

There was no reply, though the victim could be gagged, unconscious, or dead. She motioned toward the first car. "Open it."

Lyons used a scanner to imitate the car's fob, searching for the frequency. The doors clicked as the locks disengaged.

And nothing blew up.

Always a bonus.

"Pop the trunk."

Lyons did then stepped forward, lifting the lid and shaking his head. "Empty."

"Try the other one."

Lyons repeated the process then cursed as the second trunk proved empty as well.

Tanner sighed, activating her comms. "Control, Echo-Zero-One. Both target vehicles are empty, over."

"Copy that, Zero-One. Ground team on the way to relieve you. We have a new destination for you. Coordinates being relayed to your helo. Control, out."

She frowned. Control sounded disappointed.

Very disappointed.

I wonder if he knows one of them.

Fairfax Towers

Falls Church, Virginia

Kane scrolled through the security camera footage from his apartment building's lobby and elevator as his super, the rather diminutive and oxymoronically nicknamed Titanic leaned over him.

Titanic jabbed a finger at the screen, four Asian men entering with a trolly filled with supplies. "Is that them?"

"Yup." Kane took several stills of their faces then sent them to Leroux.

"You sure you don't want me to call the police?"

Kane shook his head as he rose, closeups of all ten men involved now in the hands of his friend's team. "No, I'll take care of it." He shook his phone. "This is a buddy at the FBI. He's handling it personally. If the locals get involved, it'll just mean paperwork and bureaucratic bullshit that will delay things." He slapped Titanic on the back. "Once this is finished, a box of Omaha Steaks is on me."

Titanic grinned. "I think you're my new favorite tenant."

Kane chuckled. "I bet you say that to all the guys who offer you steak."

He returned to his apartment and geared up while plotting his next move, coming up empty. This was a waiting game, and he had to wait for Leroux and his team to find something he could act on.

His phone vibrated on the dresser. He swiped his thumb, answering Leroux's call.

"Found something."

Operations Center 2, CIA Headquarters

Langley, Virginia

Leroux watched the bodycam footage as Echo Team lifted off from the Walmart parking lot, the ground team securing the area and beginning to process the cars for evidence. The van from the abduction had been traced to the cargo area of Dulles International Airport, but a malfunctioning set of cameras had made any transfer impossible to trace. When the cameras had come back online, they only showed the parked van, with no evidence anyone was inside.

Just like Walmart.

If this was the Chinese, their intel was excellent.

And Child's expert fingers had just confirmed their possible involvement, as facial patterns pulled from the footage Kane had provided were clear enough to start finding matches in the database.

"What have you got?" asked Kane.

"Three matches so far, all Chinese embassy staff. It looks like they were registered in Washington two weeks ago."

"And the others?"

"Nothing yet, but we're still working on it."

"Well, it's enough to confirm what we thought. The Chinese have found Fang, and they're taking her home."

Leroux frowned. "What are we going to do?"

"Keep tracking them. We're less than an hour behind them. Find out if there were any flights out of the airport going to China or thereabouts. Probably a charter. Depending on their flight path, we might be able to intercept them."

"That will take some doing."

"Then do it!" snapped Kane.

Leroux ignored his friend's curt reply. "I'll talk to the Chief. What are you going to do?"

"Go to the airport."

"I've already got a team heading there. Why don't you come in?"

"Negative. When you find something, I want to be able to act on it. If I'm at Langley, someone might try to stop me."

Leroux lowered his voice. "Dylan, we have to be careful."

"To hell with that," growled Kane. "I'm not stopping until I get her back. Both of them." There was a pause. "And if she dies, every last one of them is dead. Orders be damned."

Dulles International Airport

Tanner cursed as her team confirmed what she already suspected. The van was empty. Of course it was. It had been here almost an hour before they arrived.

Another perfectly executed part of what was so far a flawless operation.

As far as she could tell.

She and her team were being sent all over hell's creation with little to no intel. For all she knew, the hostiles' plan could be falling apart around them.

Yet she'd be the last to know.

A woman in coveralls that identified her as airport staff approached. "Are you in charge?"

Tanner wasn't so sure. "Yes."

"I saw something."

Her interest was piqued. "What?"

The woman pointed at the van, now being searched by her team. "When that van arrived, I saw two men get out of another van that was parked over there." She pointed to an empty spot nearby. "They carried a box that looked sort of like a coffin out of this one and put it in the back of the one that was already here, then left."

"Could you describe them?"

She shrugged. "Dunno. Chinese? Japanese? They all look the same to me."

"Uh-huh. What about the van?"

Another shrug. "Looked a lot like that one. They all look the same to me."

I'm sensing a theme.

"Color?"

The woman scratched her chin. "Black. No! Dark gray. Had something written on the side, but I don't remember what. I think it was a company name, because there was a phone number under it." She gave Tanner a look. "And no, I don't remember the number."

"How long ago was this?"

"I was on my coffee break, so, I dunno, less than an hour ago."

"Thanks." Tanner pointed at Lyons. "Go give him your contact information in case we have more questions for you."

The woman nodded and sauntered over to Lyons as Tanner contacted Control. "Control, Echo-Zero-One. We're looking for a dark gray or black van, similar to the one we tracked here. It would have left approximately an hour ago. Possibly a company name and phone number written on the side, over."

"Copy that, Zero-One, we're on it. We have another target for you. Details sent to your helo. Control, out."

Why do I feel like we're chasing our tail here?

Operations Center 2, CIA Headquarters
Langley, Virginia

Sonya Tong smiled as she examined the footage one of her team had just sent to her station. She turned to Leroux. "I've got a van that matches the description, leaving the airport about forty minutes ago."

"Track it."

Child spun his chair, his head leaning back as he stared at the ceiling. "Sounds like we're getting closer. We were an hour behind a few minutes ago."

Leroux rose. "I'm going to update the Chief."

Tong watched Leroux leave the operations center, her eyes lingering on the door. She had been infatuated with him at one point. She wasn't sure why. He was handsome enough, especially now that Sherrie had shown the poor guy how to dress properly and comb his hair, but it wasn't his looks.

It was *him*.

He had been so shy, so vulnerable, so nerdy.

49

Just like her.

She wanted to save him, and for him to save her from her loneliness.

For she was lonely.

Being a senior analyst at the CIA was time-consuming. Exhausting. It left little time to meet people socially, though that was just an excuse. Even if she had an empty calendar, she would never willingly fill it. Her life was books, television, movie trivia. She was a nerd, and was comfortable with that.

To a point.

Like anyone, she longed for someone to share her life with, to snuggle with on a Sunday evening, to go out to dinner and a movie on a Friday night.

Maybe she was kidding herself into thinking she was content with her current situation. How many nights did she sit at home, curled into a ball, sobbing at how lonely she was? How many nights did she pray for someone, anyone, to knock on her door and hold her?

When Leroux had been promoted and became her supervisor, he had become forbidden fruit, the fantasy of being with him firing up her imagination on those lonely nights. He was someone within reach, much like her, that was perhaps attainable, the only reason they weren't together the rules.

Yet Sherrie had ruined all of that for her, and for a time she resented her for it.

Though that was in the past.

Mostly.

She still carried a torch for Leroux, yet it only simmered now.

Though if Sherrie were no longer in the picture, she'd take that chance.

She silently chastised herself at the thought. Sherrie was missing, possibly dead, and here she was already planning to move in on the poor woman's man.

"I've got a possible plane," said Marc Therrien, part of her team. "Private charter heading for Shanghai. They didn't leave long ago. They were delayed taking off."

Child turned his chair to face Therrien. "I thought we weren't looking for a plane anymore. I thought everyone was in the gray van?"

Tong shook her head. "No, you're forgetting that we have the two drivers of the cars at Walmart, and we know either Sherrie or Fang was in the trunk of one of them. That's three possibles that could be on that plane. Also, we don't know if the witness is reliable. For all we know, she could be lying or mistaken. This was a well-planned op. If I wanted to throw us off the scent, I'd put a witness on the scene to distract us."

Child frowned. "Should we be running her?"

"Absolutely."

"But Chris didn't—"

Tong cut him off. "He's distracted."

"So he's making mistakes?"

"I didn't say that. We're a team, and he can't be expected to think of everything."

Child flushed. "You're right. I didn't mean—"

"I know you didn't." She sighed. "Let's just help him a little more than we usually do, okay?"

Nods rounded the room.

"Good." She smacked her hands together like Leroux would. "Now, get me everything you can on that plane and who's on it, and everything on that witness. My gut doesn't compare to Chris', but I find it kind of convenient that the only witness to the exchange just happened to be hanging around, waiting for our people to show up, and now we're supposed to be chasing a very specific van instead of paying attention to the airport."

Director Morrison's Office, CIA Headquarters
Langley, Virginia

"What's the status?"

Leroux dropped into a chair opposite Morrison's desk. "We found the two cars and the van that carried the initial team, and what we believe were used to take Sherrie and Fang from the scene. All were empty and forensics has found nothing of significance so far."

Morrison tapped his finger on his chin. "I doubt they'll lead to anything. This was well planned."

Leroux agreed. "An eyewitness claims she saw a transfer from the van we tracked to the airport to another van that was waiting. We're tracing it now."

"Is the witness reliable?"

Leroux paused. "I...assume so, but you're right, we should check her out."

Morrison frowned. "I think you're too close to this. It's not like you to miss something like that."

Leroux's shoulders slumped. "You're right. I shouldn't have, but…"
He sighed. "Maybe you should take me off this. It's already against
procedure for me to be involved."

Morrison shook his head. "No. You're the best I've got, and when
you're motivated, nobody can stop you. But take Sonya aside and make
sure she feels free to cover your ass."

"You're right. I will." His phone vibrated and he quickly scanned the
message.

"Anything important?"

Leroux chuckled. "It looks like Sonya's already covering my ass, sir.
We might have to force a private charter down."

"Explain."

"We're tracking anything that might have left the airport around the
same time as that van arrived."

Morrison's eyes narrowed. "I thought they transferred to a second
van?"

"We're still considering both possibilities, but it looks like Sonya was
suspicious of the witness like you were. She's looking into her while still
tracking the van, and the team is continuing to look into planes leaving
around the same time as the van arrived. Looks like there might be a
match."

"How confident are they?"

"Not very yet."

Morrison leaned back in his chair. "I can't get the Pentagon to force
a civilian plane to land without some sort of proof beyond a hunch."

Leroux rose. "Then I'll get you what you need."

Annandale Road, Falls Church, Virginia

"This is ridiculous."

Lyons agreed with Tanner. "You're preaching to the choir. Four vehicles tracked, four vehicles empty, and again, no cameras operating to catch any transfers."

Tanner leaned against the rear wall of a strip mall in Falls Church, back where this fiasco had all started. "This is professional. *Very* professional. As good as I've ever seen."

"Who do you think's behind it?"

"Well, that witness said they all looked Asian."

"Chinese?"

Tanner picked at her closely trimmed nails. "They'd definitely have the capability. I can't see the North Koreans being able to pull something like this off."

Lyons frowned. "If it is the Chinese, whoever they took is hooped."

"It's a long road to China."

"Not if they head east."

Tanner dismissed the idea. "They wouldn't go east. They run the risk of us finding out what plane they're on long before they can reach Chinese airspace."

Lyons thought for a moment. "True, but if they go the polar route, they could be over Russia before we find out, and it's not like the Rooskies will do anything about it."

Tanner frowned. "You're right. Let's hope Langley finds out something a little more current. We can't keep showing up after the fact. We need to catch up before it's too late."

Dulles International Airport

Kane flashed his Homeland ID to one of the officers securing the scene. "Where's the witness?"

The woman jerked a thumb over her shoulder. "Over there."

He peered past her, finding no one but police and various other agencies. "There's nobody there."

"Huh?" The officer turned to confirm it for herself. "Huh. Well, I don't know then. She was there a little while ago. I distinctly heard one of the agents tell her to wait."

"Okay, I'm going to look around." Kane quickly searched the area, confirming the witness was nowhere to be found, his suspicions, already raised, now fully red-flagged. He approached the agent in charge, flashing his ID. "I'm looking for the witness."

The man turned to point then cursed. "Son of a bitch. I told her to wait over there. I had more questions for her."

"Did you check her ID?"

"Yes." He pointed at another agent. "Check with Riggs. He wrote everything down."

"Thanks." Kane introduced himself then jotted down the information Riggs had recorded. "Did you check her out?"

Riggs nodded. "We're running her now. Nothing's come back yet that's out of the ordinary."

"Okay, thanks." Kane entered the building, dialing Leroux. "Anything for me?"

"Not yet. We've got a plane we're looking into. Private charter heading for Shanghai. Left not too long ago."

"So you're thinking this witness was too good to be true as well?"

"Actually, Sonya picked up on it." There was a pause. "I've been a little, umm, distracted." Leroux lowered his voice. "I'm not exactly at the top of my game."

Kane felt for his friend. They were all hurting, which was why normally they wouldn't be allowed to participate. He was convinced the only reason Morrison was tolerating it was for the fact the man knew they'd ignore any orders to the contrary. "We're all distracted. Just keep positive. Until I see bodies, they're both alive. Now, what can you tell me about this witness? Oh, and send me directions to the administration offices for the airport." His phone vibrated with a map a moment later.

"Done. She checks out. Clean record, worked at the airport for two years, no obvious ties to the Chinese or any other foreign government."

"Send me her file."

"Sending it now."

His phone vibrated with the secure message. "Good. Keep me posted on that plane."

"You can count on it."

Operations Center 2, CIA Headquarters

Langley, Virginia

Morrison briskly entered the operations center and Leroux rose from his station. "Anything on that plane? I've given the Pentagon a heads-up. They've scrambled jets from the DC Combat Air Patrol, but they want some evidence before they're willing to commit."

Leroux shook his head. "Nothing yet. Everything keeps checking out."

"Do we have footage of who got on?"

Leroux turned to Tong who shook her head. "No, sir, I'm afraid not."

Morrison looked askance at her. "What do you mean? There are hundreds of cameras there. It's an airport."

"I know, but we can't get access. There's some sort of block. I've talked to their techs and it's some sort of communications error. They're working on it."

Leroux pursed his lips. "Quite the coincidence, don't you think?"

Morrison frowned. "I don't believe in coincidences."

"Neither do I." Leroux turned to Child. "What kind of equipment do they have there?"

Child's eyes narrowed. "What do you mean?"

"I mean servers, communications infrastructure. Who's the manufacturer?"

Child worked his terminal then spun in his chair. "You'll never guess who did their latest upgrade last year."

Morrison cursed. "You're telling me that one of our country's most important airports is using Chinese equipment?"

"Yup."

Leroux chewed his cheek. "Now *that* can't be a coincidence."

Morrison growled. "This is *exactly* why we warned against this. Using anything Chinese beyond a kitchen blender is insanity. Don't these idiots in DC realize that absolutely *all* Chinese companies, whether public or private, in order to operate have to agree to do whatever is asked of them by the Chinese government? It's Article Seven of their damned National Intelligence Law. Yet we allow their equipment to be used in our country? These people are our enemy, and through ignorance or political correctness gone mad, we're actually considering letting them help build our 5G infrastructure." Morrison headed for the door. "Keep working on that footage, but I think we've got enough to go on to at least convince the Pentagon we're not sending them on a wild goose chase."

Administrative Office

Dulles International Airport

"She clocked out about fifteen minutes ago. Says here she wasn't feeling well."

Kane frowned. "Is she still here?"

The personnel supervisor checked the computer. "The last time her pass was used, it was to enter the women's locker room."

"Take me there."

The man's eyes bulged. "You can't go in there! You're a dude!"

Kane held up his Homeland ID. "This is an all-access pass." He gestured toward the myriad of personnel behind the counter. "Send a female employee with me if you have to, but lives depend on me talking to her before she leaves."

The man frowned but waved at one of the women behind him. "Go with him."

She gave her supervisor a look, clearly not pleased with the babysitting job. "Fine." She finally noticed Kane. "Damn fine!"

She rounded the counter and led Kane toward the locker rooms. "Damn, honey, I wouldn't mind if you walked in on me. You're gorgeous, baby."

Kane chuckled. "Sorry, I'm taken."

"I don't see no ring on that finger. If your woman loves you so much, she should mark her territory." She gave him another once over. "Now, if you were my man, I'd have a ring on that finger and my name tattooed across that cute booty of yours." She swiped her pass to the locker room. "Wait here so I make sure everyone is decent." She winked. "Not everyone is as openminded as I am."

Kane nodded but blocked the door from closing with his foot so he could hear what was going on. His escort reappeared and waved him in.

"Is she here?"

His escort shook her head, leading him to a woman tying her shoes. "She says she just left a few minutes ago."

Kane cursed. "Does she have a car?"

The woman finished tying one of her shoes with a tug. "No, I don't think so. I think she takes the bus."

Operations Center 2, CIA Headquarters

Langley, Virginia

"I'm in!" announced Child with both arms extended toward the ceiling, his chair spinning in victory.

"Good. Get me any footage from that parking garage or the plane."

"Give me a minute." Child attacked his keyboard when Tong gasped. "Look!"

Leroux turned to see her pointing at the displays at the front of the room. "What?"

"The plane. It's gone."

Leroux's eyes widened as he strode toward the displays. "What?"

"We're no longer tracking it."

He stared at the screens, his hands on his hips. "Did it go down?"

"No, it just disappeared. One minute it was there, the next it wasn't."

"Check with NORAD. See if they have it on their scopes." He turned to Tong. "And get me the Chief. There's no way us getting access to the footage, and their transponder going dark isn't connected." He jabbed a finger at the screen. "That plane is definitely involved."

Unknown Location

Sherrie woke, her head throbbing, her entire body afire with pain. She was getting worse. If she didn't get to a hospital soon, she'd be dead. And the thought filled her with an overwhelming sadness. Not for herself, but for Leroux. He would be lost without her, and she couldn't let that happen.

Not while an ounce of strength remained.

Voices in the distance had her straining to hear what was being said. She couldn't make out the words, but they sounded calm. And was that traffic? Could she be outside?

She forced her swollen eyes open and spotted a sliver of light just above her, to her left. She reached up, the effort excruciating, and pushed against what must be the lid of whatever she was inside, but could barely budge it before her arm dropped, her energy spent.

"Help!" she cried, but it was barely a hoarse whisper.

Try again!

She steeled herself then reached up once again, her goal changed, for there was no possible way she was lifting the heavy lid above her. Instead, she pushed her hand through the narrow opening, then passed out from the torturous pain.

Dulles International Airport

Kane held his phone in front of him as he memorized their witness' face, running beside the buses as they lined up, some pulling away as he raced down the platform, his escort at his side, adding a second set of eyes.

"That's her!"

Kane looked to see where his escort was pointing, and spotted their target taking a seat on one of the buses as it pulled away. He sprinted toward the front door then hammered on the glass, scaring the shit out of the driver who floored the gas. Kane pressed his ID against the glass and the driver jammed on the brakes in a panic, opening the door.

Kane boarded, flashing the poor man a smile. "Thanks. I'll just be a moment." He headed down the aisle. "Everyone remain calm, I'm with Homeland Security. This will only take a moment of your time. There's no danger." He stopped in front of his witness who pulled her earphones out. "Are you Soledad Martínez?"

She paled. "Yes."

He held up his ID. "Come with me."

Unknown Location

Fang's head pounded, her mind a fog of confusion as she slowly woke from being gassed. She struggled to focus, to cut through the white noise of her impaired mind, and suddenly everything came back into focus with a rush.

She was still in her coffin, still bound and gagged, though no longer at the airport—the sound of jets and the smell of fuel was gone.

And she wasn't in an airplane.

The familiar drone she would expect wasn't there. Instead, there was nothing. No engine sounds whatsoever. Had they just left her somewhere? Was she awake sooner than expected? Was she now alone, waiting to be picked up like an innocent package, to be delivered back to China by some international courier company unaware of what the package contained?

Her stomach fluttered as she was suddenly lifted, by whom she couldn't know, yet she had to take the chance, despite the gag.

"Help! I'm in here!"

"Shut up!" was the reply, again in Chinese.

Her heart sank as the false hope she had a moment ago was shattered. She was still a captive of those who had taken her, and her confusion grew as she wondered why she wasn't on an airplane back to China.

She gasped as her coffin was dropped unceremoniously, then she strained to listen to a conversation nearby.

"Confirm the orders."

There was a pause. "They're confirmed. Proceed."

"General Zhang Quanguo thanks you for your service, bitch."

Her mind raced. General Zhang? She knew who he was, of course. He was one of the most powerful men in China. He had brought order to Tibet, and was now doing the same, ruthlessly, in western China. Yet she had never dealt with him. Never had any involvement with him whatsoever in her entire career, nor did she know anyone who had.

I thought this had to do with the coup!

The sound of liquid pouring from a container sent her heart racing as the fumes reached her nostrils—gas, or some sort of accelerant.

What it was didn't matter.

What was about to happen did.

"Time to pay your debt!"

The air outside gasped as the fuel was lit, the smell of burning wood reaching her nostrils.

And she screamed.

"No! Please! Let me out!"

Laughter was the response.

"Please! I'll do anything you want! Please just shoot me! Don't let me die like this! Please!"

Tears filled her eyes then poured down her cheeks as she struggled as hard as she could to break free of her bonds. But it was no use—the space was simply too confined to gain any sort of leverage.

She could feel the heat now, the smell overwhelming her. She closed her eyes and steadied her breathing as she realized her pleas were falling on the ears of those who merely delighted in her terror. Instead, she denied them the satisfaction and lay as calmly as she could manage, picturing those she loved.

Her parents.

Her grandparents.

Her brother and sisters.

Sherrie.

Chris.

And Dylan.

Oh, Dylan! I'm so sorry!

She sighed as the smell of smoke surrounded her. And as she took her final breaths before the agony to come, she smiled in satisfaction in knowing those responsible would pay.

For she knew the man she loved.

And he would stop at nothing to ensure justice was delivered.

Brutally.

Operations Center 2, CIA Headquarters
Langley, Virginia

"This is Falcon-One. Five minutes to intercept, over."

Leroux sat at his station as they listened in on the Pentagon operation, his team only observers of the interception of the aircraft they had found. An aircraft they still couldn't confirm was involved. Again, miraculously, the cameras showing the plane's boarding malfunctioned for the crucial minutes that might have provided them with desperate answers.

And it was that miraculous timing that had him convinced this aircraft was absolutely involved.

At least his gut was convinced, and that was usually enough for him and the powers that be.

Tong broke the tense silence filling the room. "We've found the gray van."

Leroux tore his eyes away from the screen. "Where?"

"It went into an abandoned warehouse in Fairfax. Should I dispatch Echo Team?"

"Yes."

Tong sent the order. "Oh, this is odd."

Leroux detected the concern in her voice, giving her his full attention. "What?"

"There's already a local emergency call to that location."

Leroux tensed. "What kind of call?"

Tong looked at him, pale. "Fire."

Over Fairfax, Virginia

"Ma'am, you're going to want to see this."

Tanner rose from her seat and leaned into the cockpit, staring down at the scene below. And cursed. All manner of emergency personnel were already swarming the area including police, fire, and paramedics. "I'm guessing we're too late." She pointed at an empty area away from the action. "Set us down there. No need to alarm anyone."

"Roger that."

She sat back down. "This place is swarming with LEOs. Everyone stay with the chopper. Mike, you're with me."

Lyons grinned. "Expecting trouble?"

"I seem to remember the last time there was trouble, it was *me* who bailed *you* out."

Lyons shrugged. "What can I say? I can't hold my liquor. You all knew that going into that pub crawl."

The chopper landed as the team laughed at the memory. Tanner and Lyons hopped out and she surveyed the area, her eyes settling on a notorious British sportscar parked all alone in the sketchy parking lot. "He's brave."

Lyons glanced over at the pristine automobile. "Not really. Even the thieves know not to bother. It's liable to break down as they're making their getaway."

Tanner chuckled. "If it isn't already."

They strode toward the active scene, the fire crews still operating hoses inside the large warehouse. A police officer approached and they showed their Homeland IDs.

"Homeland? What are you guys doing here?"

"It's a national security matter." Tanner gestured toward the warehouse, smoke still billowing out the shattered windows. "What's the situation?"

"We had reports of smoke. They found a van inside on fire. The fire guys say some sort of accelerant was used. They're having a hard time putting it out."

"Anybody inside?"

"If there was, they're dead now. One of our guys thinks he spotted a foot, but we haven't confirmed that yet. Once the fire's out, we'll know more."

Tanner nodded. "Okay, let me know as soon as we can get a look. A forensics team will be here shortly."

The officer's interest was piqued, his eyebrows shooting up. "Any idea who it is? If Homeland is involved, it must be important."

Tanner chuckled. "Buddy, I only work here. Do you think the guys in Washington tell me anything?"

The officer laughed. "Happy to hear it's the same all over."

Tanner headed for the chopper, activating her comms. "Control, Echo-Zero-One. We might have a body, over."

Security Holding Room
Dulles International Airport

Kane sat across from an unconvincingly defiant Soledad Martínez. Though her folded arms and pronounced scowl indicated attitude, her hopping foot and constant fidgeting suggested otherwise.

This woman was scared.

Kane pointed toward the camera in the corner of the room. "I asked them to turn it off. Do you want to know why?"

Soledad shrugged, saying nothing.

He held up his Homeland ID. "See this?"

A glance, and again nothing.

"This says I'm Homeland Security." He put it on the table. "You wanna know something no one else knows?"

Another shrug.

"I'm *not* Homeland Security. This ID is bullshit."

Her eyes widened for a moment.

"Do you know what that means?"

She looked away, staring at the camera, as if hoping there was someone else watching.

"It means that the rules don't apply to me like they do for most people." He leaned forward. "And here's another thing. The person I'm looking for is my girlfriend. She's the only woman I have ever loved. And do you know what a person like me does to people who get in my way?"

She paled slightly, her lip trembling.

"I think you do." Kane leaned back in his chair. "Now, I'm going to ask this once, and only once. If I have to ask a second time, I'm going to leave this room, then the next time we meet, I won't be so...pleasant."

A dripping sound followed by the smell of urine confirmed his message had gotten through.

"Speak."

And she did, the verbal diarrhea rapid. "I-I didn't have a choice! I'm sorry, but I didn't."

He remained silent, letting her speak freely, his experience showing once someone started to spill what they knew, his talking would only get in the way.

There would be plenty of time for that.

"I was out for drinks with some friends a couple of weeks ago. I went out behind the bar to have a garden party, then some man approached me. He flashed me his badge, said he was FBI, and that if he reported what he had seen, I'd lose my job." She leaned forward, pleading with him. "I can't afford to lose my job! I have a kid at home and a deadbeat ex-husband. I *need* this job!"

Kane remained silent. His phone vibrated with a message. He checked it, feigning disinterest with what the woman was saying, spurring her on with the fear she wasn't telling him enough to avoid a torturous end at a later date.

CAP interception in two minutes.

He suppressed a smile. They might have Fang shortly, or perhaps Sherrie. His preference was obvious and selfish, though he wasn't going to apologize for human nature. He hoped for his friend's sake both of them were safe and sound, on board the aircraft. He just prayed whoever had them didn't decide it was better to kill them and face the consequences, rather than hand them over alive and face lesser charges.

If it was the Chinese, their operatives were fanatical enough to die for their cause. It wasn't a religious motivation like an Islamist, though it was in a way. The Communist doctrine had been drummed into them since birth, their entire education system designed to not only teach them the fundamentals that some would say the American education system had failed to do with its own children, but to also indoctrinate them into the system they lived under.

Then there was the ultimate motivation.

Do what we tell you, or your family pays the price.

"Are you even listening to me?"

Kane continued to stare at his phone. "When you say something interesting, I might."

She threw her hands up in frustration. "Well, what do you want to know?"

"You already know the answer to that." He put his phone down on the table. "I'm getting bored, and you're clearly not motivated. I think I'll be leaving now."

She reached across the table, grabbing his arm, panic on her face. "No! Wait! Listen, he gave me a choice. Either he reported me, or I did what he asked."

Kane no longer had time to toy with her. "And that was?"

"He said I'd get a phone call within a few weeks. I actually got it this morning. He told me to do what the person on the phone asked me to."

"And that was?"

"To have my cigarette break in the parking garage. A specific spot, right where you guys found that van. I was to watch what happened, then when you guys arrived, tell them what I saw, then say I was too sick to finish my shift. I was supposed to leave then take a few days off."

Kane stared at her. "You're forgetting something."

"What?"

"What did he pay you?"

Her shoulders slumped. "How did you know?"

"Because a woman like you, desperate for money with a child at home and a deadbeat ex-husband, doesn't just take a few days off without pay. And"—he pointed at a shiny new watch on her wrist—"a woman like you, desperate for money, doesn't wear a brand new five-hundred-dollar watch."

Her jaw dropped, then snapped shut after a few moments. She sighed. "Fine. Ten grand. Cash."

"When?"

"That night."

"So, he was prepared when he met you."

Her eyes narrowed. "What do you mean?"

"It doesn't matter." Yet it did. It meant everything. It meant it wasn't a chance encounter, it was a planned encounter. They knew she'd be there that night, they knew exactly who she was, where she worked, and that she was a habitual marijuana smoker, a fireable offense they could blackmail her with.

Again, perfectly planned, and it meant access to personnel files of a federally run organization.

"Would you recognize him?"

She shook her head. "No, it was an alleyway at night. He was in the shadows the whole time."

"White? Black?"

"He was Asian. That much I could tell."

Kane pursed his lips. "Anything else you're not telling me?"

"No."

"Are you sure? If I find out later that you're lying to me—"

"No! I swear that's it. I've told you everything."

Kane stood. "You can go."

Her eyes bulged. "Umm, I can?"

"Yes."

"Umm, what about the money."

Kane's eyes bore into her. "Return the watch, and spend it all on your kid."

Operations Center 2, CIA Headquarters
Langley, Virginia

Leroux stared at the various feeds monitoring the intercept of the private jet then rose from his station as Morrison entered the operations center.

"Report."

"Sir, the plane is approaching Canadian airspace and is not responding to hails."

Morrison joined him at the center of the room, taking in the information displayed in front of him. "What are the Canadians doing?"

"They've scrambled F-18s from CFB Bagotville to intercept."

Morrison shook his head, staring at the map. "Why didn't they go out to sea? At least they'd be in international waters, then they could have gone north and taken the polar route."

"No idea. Right now, they're on a standard flight plan matching the one they filed. No deviations. If it weren't for their transponder going silent, there'd be nothing suspicious about their flight. According to

Dulles, they departed without incident, though had been delayed due to a backlog after an equipment malfunction in the luggage handling area."

"When was it booked?"

"Two weeks ago, according to the charter company."

"Do we know who's on board?"

Child brought up the manifest, the passport information for the crew and passengers displayed. "Three crew, four Chinese businessmen."

"Have we run them?"

Leroux nodded. "Yes. They're clean as far as we can tell."

"So, they might not even know they have our people on board."

Child grunted. "Or they're doing a favor for their Chinese overlords."

Leroux agreed with both possibilities. "Anything is possible. I doubt the pilot knows, however. He shows as a Swedish citizen, and his co-pilot is French."

Tong interrupted. "Sir, our fighters are reporting the pilot is visually indicating a comms failure. He's turning now."

Morrison headed for the door. "Good. Maybe we'll have some answers when they land. Send Echo Team."

Leroux returned to his station. "Yes, sir."

"Sirs!" exclaimed Tong, excitement in her voice.

Everyone turned toward her, Morrison halting his exit. "What?" asked Leroux.

"They found one of them!"

Walmart Supercenter, Kings Crossing

Arlington, Virginia

Sherrie woke to the sounds of voices. Loud voices. They were all around her, no longer in the distance. Hands grabbed her and a shot of panicked adrenaline rushed through her system, giving her a momentary burst of energy as she struggled to fight them off.

Yet the fight was short-lived, the energy fleeting.

"Calm down. You're safe now."

The voice was soothing, concerned.

English.

No more Chinese.

She was lifted into the air then placed on something softer, more comfortable than the confines she had been trapped in for so long.

"She's suffered severe trauma. It looks like they laid quite the beating on her."

"You should see them," she whispered, the laughter buoying her spirits, finally confirming to her that she truly had been rescued.

Someone patted her shoulder. "That's good. Keep up that sense of humor. It means your old noggin is still working."

"She took a blow to the back of the head," said another. "Looks pretty bad." The person leaned in, though her swollen eyes didn't let her see them beyond a shadow on the other side of her eyelids. "Do you have a headache?"

"Like a college hangover. It hursh ev…where." Her heart raced at her slurred speech, and her newly discovered world faded.

"We're losing her!"

En route to Walmart Supercenter, Kings Crossing
Arlington, Virginia

Kane raced toward the Walmart Leroux had notified him of only minutes before. He had already been heading back to Langley when he had received the call, and he had broken pretty much every traffic law imaginable since. At the moment, he knew nothing beyond someone had been found at the scene of the two abandoned cars used in the abduction.

How whoever it was had been missed for so long he had no idea, but heads would roll if Fang or Sherrie died because of it.

He spotted the Walmart ahead, a beehive of law enforcement activity, an ambulance just pulling out onto the road, its siren wailing, its lights flashing as a police escort cleared the way.

He followed, drafting the ambulance to take advantage of the cleared path.

He instructed the car to dial Leroux. "What do we know?"

A clearly distraught Leroux replied. "J-just that her heart stopped. That's all I know. I don't know if they got it going again."

"I'm behind the ambulance now. Do we know who it is? Is it Fang or Sherrie?"

"No. I'm trying to find out but there was no ID."

Kane slammed his palm into the steering wheel. "Hell, was she Asian or Caucasian?"

"I-I didn't think…"

Kane could hear his friend's anguish, and his own emotions threatened to get the best of him. He drew a calming breath, determined to avoid taking his frustrations out on his best friend. "It's okay, buddy, we're all messed up and not thinking straight. Tell Sonya to ask them if the victim is Asian or Caucasian."

"Just-just a second."

He heard a burst of static then Tong's voice replaced Leroux's. "Hi Dylan, this is Sonya. I'm taking over for a few minutes."

"Understood. Is he okay?"

There was a pause. "No," replied Tong in a whisper, her own voice cracking. "Are you?"

Kane gripped the steering wheel a little tighter. "Not yet. Did you find out—"

"She's Caucasian. I'm—I'm sorry, Dylan, I know that's not what you wanted to hear."

Kane's shoulders slumped, angered at it not being Fang, then overwhelmed with guilt at treating Sherrie's life as less valuable than his girlfriend's. He struggled to control his anguish. "Tell the Chief to send Chris to the hospital. Send a security detail as well." His ears pounded with a realization. "If Sherrie's in that ambulance, then those remains they found…"

"We don't know that yet, Dylan. Echo Team is about to enter that jet. She may be on board."

Kane's heart hammered as tunnel vision threatened to take control. He steadied his breathing and released the death grip he had on the wheel. "Keep me posted."

Joint Base McGuire–Dix–Lakehurst

Tanner sprinted toward the airplane, her team on her heels as scores of troops and vehicles surrounded the private charter. The door opened and the stairs dropped, a military team taking the lead on this one, approaching the aircraft and ordering the occupants out.

A group of terrified men and women emerged, hands raised, the action over within minutes. As the passengers were patted down and their IDs checked, a team boarded the aircraft, a rapid search conducted for any stragglers or kidnap victims. The officer in charge exited the plane, shaking his head.

The cargo holds were opened and emptied as Tanner approached the pilot, his hands cuffed behind his back. She flashed her badge. "Tanner. Homeland Security. Was anything loaded in the last few minutes before takeoff?"

"Just their carry-ons. Their luggage was loaded about half an hour before we taxied."

"Anything else on board? Anything your company was filling any excess capacity with?"

He shook his head. "Not that I'm aware of. We're not a cargo aircraft. You're right, sometimes we courier stuff if we know there's going to be excess capacity, but this flight has nothing like that on board."

"Nothing large, like a…coffin?"

The pilot's eyebrows popped. "Just what is it you're looking for?"

"Answer the question."

"No, just standard luggage."

"Mind if we open everything up?"

The man eyed her. "You just had fighter jets force me to the ground. If you can do that, I think you can do whatever the bloody hell you want. But when you get to my suitcase, somebody get a fresh pair of underwear for me. I think I shit myself earlier."

Tanner chuckled. "I don't blame you."

"What the hell is this about? Why are you bringing my plane down just because of a comms failure?"

"Your transponder was turned off, and you left Dulles immediately after an…incident, shall we say?"

"You mean you think we're involved in some sort of terrorist plot?"

"It was a possibility." She watched the military personnel haul the last bag out of the hold. She stepped over to the large pile. "Open anything big enough to contain a body."

Everyone stared at her, the officer in charge approaching. "Nobody can fit in these, ma'am."

Tanner regarded him. "Not in one piece."

En route to Inova Fairfax Hospital

Falls Church, Virginia

Leroux stared ahead, his mind a fog of confusion, ignoring everything around him, the traffic a blur. Thankfully, Morrison had insisted on driving him to the hospital, playing it off as his duty since it was one of his personnel near death.

Near death.

The very thought had Leroux's stomach in knots, bile filling his mouth, his head gripped by a headache he couldn't shake.

He couldn't think straight.

Thank God for Sonya.

He was useless. He couldn't run an operation, not in his condition.

And if Sherrie dies...

If she died, it was all over. His life was over. She was everything to him. The only woman he had ever loved, the person who had dragged him, kicking and screaming, out of his shell.

She had made him into the man he was today.

And without her in his life, none of it was worth it.

A tear rolled down his cheek and he quickly wiped it away, though he was certain Morrison had seen it.

The phone rang and Morrison answered it. "This is Morrison. You're on speaker with a cleared passenger."

"Sir, this is Sonya Tong. We just heard from Echo Team. They found nothing on board. We're all of the opinion here that these people were set up."

"A diversion?"

"Yes, sir."

Leroux, dragged from his fog of emotions, stared at Morrison as a horrifying conclusion occurred to him. "If Sherrie is at the hospital, and no one is on that plane, then that must mean the remains in the van..." He couldn't say it, he couldn't acknowledge what was now obvious, for doing so meant it was true. As long as he didn't say it, it wasn't a fact, there was still a possibility.

Morrison's jaw squared. "Until I have proof, I'm not assuming anything. Miss Tong, I want to know the moment you find out anything on those remains."

"Yes, sir."

Morrison ended the call then glanced at a shaking Leroux. "How are you holding up, son?"

"Like shit, sir."

Morrison chuckled. "No doubt."

"Dylan's going to be worse. He loves Fang as much as I love Sherrie. If she's dead, he's going to go apeshit. I wouldn't want to be the Chinese tomorrow."

Morrison frowned. "I know, that's what I'm afraid of."

"Are you going to order him to stand down?"

Morrison gave him a look. "Do you think that would work?"

Leroux grunted. "Not for a second."

"Then we better make sure whoever he starts killing deserves to be killed, or we could have a bigger problem on our hands than one dead foreign operative, and one badly beaten intelligence asset."

Fairfax, Virginia

Echo Team's chopper landed gently, any urgency now gone. All that was left was the identification of the remains found in the burned-out van. And if those remains proved to be one of their victims, the day would have been a failure.

Something none of her team were pleased with.

They strode toward the scene, the last firetruck pulling away, the smoke billowing from the abandoned warehouse now gone. Police swarmed the perimeter, but inside, the warehouse was controlled by CIA personnel seconded to Homeland. She approached a tech holding some sort of gadget near a table, some of the charred remains laid out on it.

"What have you got?"

The woman looked up, then gestured with the device. "The Rapid DNA Analyzer is comparing the DNA we just pulled from the remains. We should have a result shortly."

Lyons' eyebrows popped. "That quickly?"

"Yup. State of the art. It's basically a lab on a chip."

Tanner eyeballed the machine with curiosity. "Cool. What are you comparing it to?"

"Sorry, classified."

Tanner rolled her eyes. "What else is new."

The tech chuckled. "Tell me about it. *I* don't even know who I'm testing against. All I know is that I had two samples to test against, and was just told to exclude one of them."

"What do you think that means?"

The tech shrugged. "Don't know, but one of the locals here said he heard over the radio that they recovered a badly beaten victim at a Walmart not too far from here."

Tanner felt sick and took a step back, Lyons placing a steadying hand on her arm. "Where did you say?"

"In a dumpster behind a Walmart. I don't know which one."

Tanner closed her eyes, sighing heavily. She looked at Lyons. "We should have searched the area."

Lyons shook his head. "Those weren't our orders. The ground team was supposed to, not us. We were ordered out minutes after we arrived."

The tech ignored her discomfort. "Hey, do you guys know what's going on?"

Tanner sucked in a deep breath. "Not an effin' clue, just that I've put more miles in on that chopper today than I have in months."

The device beeped in the tech's hand.

"What's that mean?"

"It means we've got a match."

Inova Fairfax Hospital

Falls Church, Virginia

Leroux climbed out of Morrison's SUV as the Chief's phone rang. His boss waved him on. "Go in, I'll take this then find you."

"Yes, sir." Leroux headed through the hospital doors and into the organized chaos an emergency department usually was. He flashed his ID to get to the front of the line. "I'm looking for a patient that was brought in. Sherrie White."

"Mr. Leroux?"

He turned to see a woman approaching. "Yes?"

"I'm Cynthia Rhodes. I was told to expect you by your office. Follow me, would you?"

He followed Rhodes to an elevator. "Is she okay?"

Rhodes frowned slightly as they boarded. "She's alive. I think it's best if the doctor explains everything. All I can tell you is that she was badly beaten, and from what I hear from the paramedics, left for dead."

Rage and fear threatened to overwhelm him and he gripped the railing, leaning against the wall, Rhodes not noticing as she faced the doors.

"She suffered severe head trauma. It looks like she was hit over the head with something. The doctor thinks she was pistol-whipped from behind, then kicked repeatedly. There were very few defensive wounds. We've had to put her in an induced coma."

The doors opened and she reached back, pulling him out after her, concern on her face. "Are you okay?"

He wiped the sweat from his forehead, his entire body weak. "Is-is she going to die?"

"I'll let the doctor—"

"Chris!"

He looked up with tear-filled eyes and spotted Kane rushing toward him. They hugged hard, and his friend led him to the window outside Sherrie's room.

And the sight had his knees buckling, only Kane's supporting arm keeping him from collapsing. She was bandaged it seemed from head to toe, with more tubes and wires coming out of her than he had ever known possible. Her eyes were swollen shut, and she was on what appeared to be a ventilator.

Kane guided him to a chair, Rhodes leaving for a moment. Kane knelt in front of Leroux. "You okay?"

Leroux shook his head. "No." He stared at his only friend. "If I lose her…"

"You won't. She's a fighter. You know that. She's the strongest woman I know with the possible exception of Fang."

Rhodes returned with a bottle of water and handed it to Leroux. "Drink this. It will make you feel better."

Leroux complied, taking several long swigs. A man walked over and Rhodes introduced him. "This is Doctor Lenze."

Leroux stood, shaking the man's hand, but couldn't speak. Thankfully, Kane took over.

"What can you tell us?"

"The next forty-eight hours will tell. She has swelling on the brain. We've induced a coma, and we're taking her in for surgery now to relieve the pressure. If she survives the next two days, then I'm confident she'll be okay."

Leroux watched as a team entered her room, moments later pushing her out.

Lenze patted Leroux on the shoulder. "I have to go. I'll see you after the surgery."

Leroux dropped back into the chair as Morrison joined them, his face grim.

And Leroux was certain he knew why.

As apparently did Kane.

His friend's fists clenched. "It's Fang, isn't it?"

Morrison placed a hand on Kane's shoulder. "I'm sorry, son, but the DNA test confirmed it. It was her remains in the van."

Kane's fists clenched harder, his jaw tight as the veins in his neck threatened to explode, his face turning red as every muscle in his body tensed.

Then he collapsed in the chair beside Leroux and let out a heart-wrenching gasp, his shoulders slumping and his head drooping as tears erupted. He gripped the arms of his chair, his knuckles turning white as his shoulders heaved. Leroux put an arm over his friend's shoulders, and for the first time he could recall, his only friend for so many years turned and hugged him, the two sobbing as they held each other.

Then, abruptly, Kane stopped, extricating himself from the embrace as he stood and faced Morrison, not bothering to wipe the tears from his face. "Request permission to take some vacation time, sir."

Morrison regarded him. "Granted. But I want you to stay in country."

Kane stared at him, saying nothing.

"I mean it, Dylan. Let us work the problem. When I have a target for you, I'll call you."

"Is that a promise?"

Morrison extended his hand and leaned in, lowering his voice and he clasped Kane's hand. "You have my word, that the people responsible for what happened today will be found, and eliminated by your hand."

Operations Center 2, CIA Headquarters
Langley, Virginia
Two weeks later

Tong sat at her customary station, having successfully avoided Leroux's these past two weeks, despite the fact she was temporarily the team's lead. They had been assigned the task of tracking down all involved in Fang's death and Sherrie's beating, Morrison demanding proof of everything before action could be taken.

And she understood his concern.

This was China they were dealing with, not North Korea or Iran, or some other despotic regime. There were only two countries in the world that concerned her from a military standpoint—Russia and China. Neither could be challenged without risking an all-out conflict that could inflict serious damage on the United States, even if Uncle Sam might ultimately win.

At what price?

She wasn't certain what the game plan was after they handed over their intel. Leroux was at Sherrie's side in the hospital on a near-constant vigil these past two weeks, Kane hadn't been heard from but was assumed to be at his apartment, and each new piece of intel simply confirmed what they already knew beyond any doubt.

China was behind this.

The private jet they had forced down had been combed from cockpit to tail, and nothing had been found. Physically. Computer forensics had confirmed that someone had hacked the system through a backdoor built into the hardware.

The Chinese hardware.

They had used the backdoor to disable the comms and the transponder, disguising the fact from the pilots who were left blissfully unaware anything was wrong until two F-16s buzzed them to get their attention.

The same was true at Dulles.

Chinese hardware, with a backdoor that had allowed them to disable cameras as needed, delete footage where necessary, access personnel files, disrupt external communications thus delaying their investigation, and delay flights so the aircraft they had chosen as the decoy took off at the last possible moment, allowing it to be the sole focus of everyone involved.

While they killed Fang, then escaped the country.

The operation was planned perfectly. Vehicle exchange points were all in camera dead zones or where the equipment allowed them to override the devices, the vehicles were all rentals, stolen off the lots the night before with fake plates printed that matched the vehicle types. That meant they had access to the DMV, a hack just confirmed yesterday.

Everything screamed professional. Government. Chinese.

As far as anyone could tell, the only thing that had gone wrong was Sherrie. They hadn't known about her, and hadn't known she was supposed to have lunch with Fang. Three of their people were dead because of the resistance the two women had raised. But resistance had been planned for, hence the cleaning crew. They had restored the apartment to near-perfect order, though had no ability to fix the bullet holes in the couch. If it weren't for that, only a trained agent like Kane would have spotted the slight imperfections.

And then there was the lone drop of blood found under the couch.

It had been discovered by the forensics team that swept the apartment later that tragic day. It had been genetically typed and shown to be Chinese, but beyond that, it was of little use. All they had were the photos of the men involved. All caught on camera in the lobby and elevator of the apartment building. The lone cameras involved that weren't accessible externally. She believed, and the others investigating this heinous crime agreed, that the Chinese had planned to come back and erase the footage, or do so on the way out, but Sherrie's interference, then Kane's return to the apartment shortly after the abduction, had prevented that.

It was the lone screw up in an otherwise perfect plan.

That, and Sherrie.

It was assumed they must have figured out who she was, either through interrogation or her equipment and tactics, and decided against killing her. Terminating an operative on domestic soil was how international incidents were created. Killing an exiled former special operator was not.

Not if it were done cleanly.

And if Fang hadn't been so intimately tied to CIA personnel, and Sherrie hadn't been physically assaulted to the point of near-death, the matter likely would be swept under the rug. The authorities knew the faces, they would be flagged, and if the Chinese were ever stupid enough to have their assassins set foot back in the United States, they'd be arrested and charged.

But that wouldn't be the case.

She had no doubt both Leroux and Kane wanted revenge, and for that, Morrison needed his answers. Answers she and the team were having trouble finding. They had names for all the faces now, all having registered at various foreign posts over the years, all for short stints, all now linked to disappearances over the years. Nobody had put it together until now. These were specialists in extraordinary rendition—specifically the return to China of those living in exile.

And that was one piece of the puzzle that still had her troubled. Why kill Fang and burn her body in the warehouse? These men specialized in extraordinary rendition, not assassination. Why would they kill her? And if that was the intent from the beginning, why not simply kill her in the apartment and leave? Why not make it look like a robbery gone bad, and be done with it?

The only theory she had at the moment was that the Sherrie element had ruined their carefully laid plans, and orders were given to eliminate

Fang rather than bring her home. It made sense. Cut your losses and get out of Dodge.

"I think I've got something."

She turned to Child. "What?"

"One of our guys just showed up in Malaysia."

Her eyes widened at what might be their first break. "Are you sure?"

"I've been tapping as many customs feeds as I can, and he arrived with three others in Kuala Lumpur two hours ago."

"I take it the other three aren't on our list?"

"No."

"Run them. See if we have anything on them. And check out who's in Kuala Lumpur that the Chinese might be interested in."

"I'm on it."

She headed for the door. "I'll let the Chief know we've finally got something actionable."

Inova Fairfax Hospital
Falls Church, Virginia

Leroux sat beside Sherrie's hospital bed, his head resting on the narrow mattress as he drifted in and out of sleep. He rarely left her side unless it was absolutely necessary, his phone was dead, he was starving, thirsty, and a mess. Outside of visiting hours, he sometimes slept in his car, other times managed to make it home, though often not for days.

He was lost.

The surgery to relieve the pressure on Sherrie's brain had been a success, and the doctors were convinced it was only a matter of time before she woke, though he could tell from the staff dealing with her, they were concerned. The efforts to convince him to talk to her grew with each day, and it was clear they weren't sure what to do anymore. He had asked if there was something they could do to speed up the process, some drug, some injection, but they said it was best if she came out of it naturally.

But what if she doesn't?

A knock at the door had him lifting his head. His eyes widened at the sight of his concerned parents in the doorway. His mother burst into tears at the sight of Sherrie, the evidence of her beating still obvious though nothing compared to what it was two weeks ago.

"Oh my God, Chris, what happened? Why didn't you tell us?"

Leroux rose and hugs were exchanged as tears rolled down his cheeks as the only other people in his life that might help him were finally there. "How did you find out?"

His father put some bags down in the corner. "I had to call your office."

Leroux frowned. "You shouldn't have done that."

"We hadn't heard from you in two weeks, and you weren't returning our calls."

His mother gave him a gentle slap on the cheek. "If we had known, we would have come right away to help."

He stared at Sherrie. "There's nothing you can do."

His mother shook her head. "Not for her, but for you there is." She stared up at him, concern on her face. "You look near death yourself. When was the last time you ate?"

He shrugged. "I don't know."

"Well, we're here now. We're going to take care of you. Let's get you home and cleaned up."

He shook his head. "I can't leave her. If—when she wakes up, I don't want her to be alone."

His father dropped into a chair in the corner. "I'll stay. You go with your mother and get cleaned up, because frankly, son, you stink. Have a shower, eat something, and get some rest in a proper bed. Come back here in the morning. Your mother and I will take shifts to make sure a familiar face is here when she wakes up."

Leroux sighed, his shoulders slumping in relieved defeat. "You're right." He gave Sherrie a kiss on the forehead. "I'll be back soon." He turned to his father. "What are you going to do?"

His father waved his eReader. "I've got a thousand good books to entertain me."

Leroux smiled. "And just think, when I got you that for Christmas, you thought it was a horrible idea."

His father shrugged. "I can admit it when I'm wrong." He jerked his head toward the door. "Now go, your stench is probably hindering her recovery."

Leroux took one last glance at Sherrie before saying a silent prayer, the pressure of the past two weeks lifting slightly with the arrival of his parents. "Thank God you guys are here."

Director Morrison's Office, CIA Headquarters

Langley, Virginia

"What should we do?"

Morrison's reply shocked Tong. "Nothing."

Her eyes bulged. "What?"

"Nothing. The White House doesn't want us to pursue it."

Tong was flabbergasted, her mind searching for the words she hadn't been prepared to find. "Why not?" she finally managed.

"Fang isn't an American citizen, and Sherrie is alive. As far as they're concerned, they don't want to risk an international incident over this. They're going to keep it in their back pocket in case one day we do something similar and get caught. We can haul this card out and play it if necessary."

"What about Chris? He's going to be devastated."

"He'll understand." Morrison frowned. "But he's not the one I'm worried about."

"You mean Dylan. Are you going to tell him?"

Morrison shook his head. "No. He'll create that international incident, even if I order him not to."

Kane/Lee Residence, Fairfax Towers
Falls Church, Virginia

Kane sat on the bullet-riddled couch, staring at the television, the screen as black as his soul. A bottle of Glen Breton Ice sat perched on one knee, no glass in sight as he took another swig straight from the bottle. He couldn't remember the last time he had eaten, nor could he remember the last time he had been hungry.

He couldn't remember much of anything.

Which was exactly the way he wanted it.

He wanted to forget. He wanted to forget what had happened, forget the pain, forget the anguish.

To forget Fang.

To forget life.

He had spoken to no one in two weeks, hadn't checked his messages, his emails, nothing. He hadn't contacted his best friend to see how Sherrie was doing, had ignored Leroux's knocks on the door in the early days, his friend thankfully giving up on him, just as Kane had given up on the world. There had been no word from work on any progress in the investigation, and his experience told him what that meant.

It meant they weren't going to do anything about it.

There was no way Langley hadn't figured out exactly who was behind this. They had their photos, and people had to travel. They knew who they were, yet were doing nothing about it.

Morrison had broken his promise.

He picked up his phone, flipping through old photos of him and Fang, the tears flowing anew, when it vibrated in his hand, the message preview appearing at the top of the screen. He was about to dismiss it when he paused, wiping away the tears.

We found one of them.

He tapped on the message and found an attachment. He put the bottle down on the table and sat up, reading the anonymous message about the man that had just arrived in Kuala Lumpur, a man he recognized from the footage he had pulled with Titanic.

One of the original six men.

One of the assassins.

His phone vibrated with another message.

Don't go doing anything stupid now.

Kane stood and headed for the bathroom.

What's stupid about going to a foreign country and torturing a man for information before killing him slowly?

Leroux/White Residence, Fairfax Towers
Falls Church, Virginia

Leroux woke to a gentle knock on his bedroom door. He rolled over in the incredibly comfortable bed, groaning at the interruption. "Yeah?"

"Dylan is here, dear."

His eyes widened at the announcement. He hadn't seen him since the revelation that Fang had died, and calls, texts, and knocks on the door had gone unanswered. Perhaps his friend was ready to face the world once again, which was good.

He wasn't so sure if he was ready himself, however.

"Give me a sec." He rose and threw on some clothes before checking himself in the mirror. He had cleaned himself up before hitting the sheets, but the black circles under his eyes betrayed the exhaustion he still felt despite sleeping for almost half a day straight.

He blasted a breath through his lips then headed for the living area, preparing for an emotional encounter that would add to his exhaustion.

And was shocked at what greeted him.

A smiling, perfectly kempt Kane.

"Hiya, buddy."

Leroux exchanged a quick thumping hug with his friend. "You look good. When I hadn't heard from you for two weeks, I thought you were, well, you know."

Kane chuckled as he took a seat. "I was, but there's nothing like the possibility of revenge to perk up a man, if you know what I mean."

Leroux's mother frowned. "What are you up to, Dylan?"

Kane grinned. "I don't think you want to know." He rose, pointing toward the bedroom. "Your son and I have something to discuss."

Leroux's mother rolled her eyes. "You two talk, but don't get my boy in trouble." She stared at Kane. "When's the last time you ate a proper meal that didn't come out of a bottle of"—she sniffed—"scotch?"

Kane shrugged. "I think I had ramen last night."

"Pfft. That's just water, some noodles, and twice the daily recommended sodium in one bowl. I'll fix you something proper."

"No time."

"Then I'll fix you a sandwich." Kane was about to say something when she jabbed the air with her finger. "And you're going to eat it, young man!"

Kane smiled. "Yes, Mrs. Leroux." He gave Leroux a sideways glance. "Does this remind you of high school, or what?"

Leroux laughed, the thoughts of those times with his friend dragging him from his funk if only for a brief moment. He led Kane to the bedroom then sat on the edge of the mattress as Kane closed the door then paced in front of the dresser.

"Your mother is a force of nature."

"Tell me about it. Now, what's going on? You said revenge?"

Kane paused, regarding his friend for a moment. "So, they didn't tell you either?"

"Tell me what?"

Kane resumed his pacing. "They found one of them in Kuala Lumpur. He just arrived a few hours ago."

Leroux tensed, unsure of how to feel. "No, they didn't tell me, though I haven't really been in the loop since, well, you know."

"Me neither, but someone wants us to know."

"Who?"

Kane shrugged. "Sonya? She's always been sweet on you. Maybe she wanted you to know."

"Then why did she tell you?"

"Because she likes you. She doesn't want you to get in trouble. By telling me, she's helping you get revenge, but I'm the one who'll get in trouble if something goes wrong."

Leroux pursed his lips, thinking. "I don't know. It doesn't sound like her."

Kane shrugged. "Well, whoever it is, it doesn't matter. We've got a limited window to act."

"What are you going to do?"

"Go get him."

Leroux's eyebrows crawled up his forehead. "But by the time you get there, he could be gone."

"Which is why I need you backing me up."

"You mean go back to the office? They'll never let me help you on a rogue op."

Kane shook his head, leaning against the dresser. "No, I want you to go to my ops center. We've done it before. You know it has everything you need."

Leroux's chin dropped to his chest, his body going limp. "I…I can't. I have to be there when Sherrie wakes up."

"Then get help."

"Who?"

"Get that Tommy kid. He proved useful and trustworthy. And I know someone else who'll help you."

"Who?"

"Sonya. If you ask her, she'll be there in a heartbeat."

"I don't want her to get in trouble."

"Who would know? And she's helped before outside of channels."

Leroux sighed. "This is insane." He stared at his friend. "And what do you intend to do if you find him?"

"Besides kill him?"

"Yeah."

"Find out where the others are so I can kill them too."

Staff Parking Garage, CIA Headquarters

Langley, Virginia

Leroux sat in his car in the underground parking garage at Langley. He hadn't been here long, which was probably a good thing. Sitting in a car alone at CIA Headquarters was bound to attract attention if it went on for too long. He knew exactly when Tong would finish her shift, and didn't want to spend any more time away from Sherrie than he had to. He spotted his underling briskly walking to her car, exactly as expected.

He rolled down his window. "Sonya!"

Tong turned then smiled at him as he waved her over. She rushed to his window, clearly happy to see him. "Chris, what are you doing here?"

He motioned toward the passenger seat. "Get in and I'll explain."

Her eyes narrowed but she joined him as he rolled up the window. "So, what's going on?"

"I hear you found one of them."

Her eyes shot wide. "How did you find out?"

"You don't know?"

She eyed him. "Is Randy feeding you information?"

Leroux was surprised at her reaction. "No, actually, I assumed it was you."

She shook her head. "It wasn't me. I wish it was. I mean, I wish I had, but there's nothing we can do with the intel, so I didn't want you worrying about things. I wanted you focusing on Sherrie."

He smiled. "I appreciate that, but unfortunately, Dylan knows, and he's not going to sit on it."

Tong's jaw dropped. "You told him?"

"Actually, he told me."

Tong went bug-eyed. "Someone told him! Who?"

He shrugged. "Well, like I said, until this conversation, we both thought it was you."

"It wasn't, I swear."

"Well, it doesn't matter. What does, is what happens now. Dylan is going after the guy, but he's going to need backup."

She shook her head. "I already talked to the Chief. We're not authorized for an op. White House orders."

"We assumed as much. I'm going to be providing backup from Dylan's own facility."

"The one in the storage containers?"

"Yes."

She stared at him for a moment. "How can I help?"

Leroux smiled. "I was hoping you were going to say something like that."

"You know I'd do anything for you...and Sherrie."

He didn't let on he knew exactly what she meant. "Of course."

She reached for the door handle. "I'll go tell the Chief that I need some time off. HR has been hounding me to chew up some of my vacation time, and with you off, our workload is fairly light. They can spare me."

"Good."

"Will anyone else be helping?"

"I'm thinking Tommy Granger."

Tong nodded. "Good choice. He knows his way around a computer, and there's nothing he doesn't know about communications." She grabbed Leroux by the wrist and squeezed. "Let's do this. Let's make sure those bastards get what's coming to them."

Granger/Trinh Residence

St. Paul, Maryland

"I know what we're doing for the next week."

Tommy Granger glanced up from his laptop at his girlfriend, Mai Trinh. "What?"

"Lost in Space seasons one and two."

A smile spread. "Season two is out?"

She grinned. "Netflix just emailed me."

"Awesome! How long has it been? Like two years?"

She shrugged. "Something stupid, but long enough that I can't remember the first season at all, so we'll have to watch it, or we'll be, you know, lost in Lost in Space."

He laughed, reaching out a hand for her. She took it and he hauled her into his lap. "My girl is getting witty!"

She gave him a kiss. "I've always been witty. You just don't speak enough Vietnamese to know it."

He laughed. "I guess you've got me there."

She repositioned, straddling his lap, then gave him a grind. "How about we stow the jokes and burn off some energy before we park ourselves in front of the TV for the rest of the weekend."

He moaned in agreement. "I say to hell with the TV. Let's watch it in the bedroom, that way we can Netflix and chill all damned weekend."

She pouted. "But then only one of us can see it."

"Not if we do it do—" His phone vibrated and he glanced at it, his eyes narrowing at his own name shown on the call display. "That's odd."

She gave him duck lips. "You're going to take a call before our sex and sci-fi marathon even begins?"

He took the call, curious who was spoofing his own number. "Hello?"

"Hi Tommy, this is Chris Leroux."

His heart raced and he bolted upright, almost tossing Mai off his lap. "Mr. Leroux! Umm, how are you?"

"Fine. I need your help again if you're available. Same pay as before, same conditions."

Tommy smiled. "When?"

"Immediately."

He glanced at a clearly annoyed Mai. "Umm, okay. Where?"

"Same rendezvous point as last time. Do you remember where that is?"

"Yes. I can be there in an hour."

Mai climbed off his lap, her displeasure clear.

"Good, I'll see you there."

The call ended and he turned to Mai to plead his case. "I have to go. Sorry."

She glared at him from the opposite end of the couch. "Who was it?"

"It was the"—he lowered his voice to a whisper—"CIA. They need my help again."

Mai's annoyance turned to concern. "Will it be dangerous?"

"Of course! It's the"—and again he whispered—"CIA."

"I don't like this."

"Do you realize how much they paid me last time? We'll be able to put that down payment on a new car. Imagine not having to constantly drag it in for repairs. You waited two hours for a tow truck last time."

"Where will you be?"

"Can't say. Classified."

"You've been dying to say that, haven't you?"

He grinned. "You have no idea."

Director Morrison's Office, CIA Headquarters

Langley, Virginia

Tong entered Morrison's office, not heading for one of the chairs in front of his desk, instead hanging by the door, one foot literally out of the room. "Umm, Chief, ahh, quick question."

Morrison looked up from his laptop. "What is it?"

"I was, umm, wondering, well, with things being so quiet around here, could I maybe take a couple of days off? Maybe a few?"

Morrison regarded her for a moment then returned his attention to his computer. "Go ahead."

"Thank you, sir."

She turned to leave when he stopped her.

"Oh, and Sonya?"

A chill rushed through her body. "Yes?"

"Stay connected, just in case we need you."

"Of course, sir."

She beat a hasty retreat back toward the parking garage, her heart hammering until she was driving through the gates of CIA Headquarters.

She had gotten away with it.

Her eyes narrowed as she pulled into traffic.

That was too easy.

She frowned as she accelerated away from one of the most secure complexes in the world. Morrison had to know what was going on—he had let her go without any questions.

Her eyes widened slightly at another possibility.

Or I'm not as essential as I think I am!

Inova Fairfax Hospital
Falls Church, Virginia

Leroux entered Sherrie's hospital room and smiled at his father, holding vigil in the corner. "Any change?"

His father shook his head. "No, I'm afraid not."

"How long have you been here?"

"Not long. Visiting hours just started. Your mother will be along shortly. She said she's doing your laundry. I think she said she's doing it twice to get the stink out properly."

He chuckled. "Well, I've got some, umm, inconvenient news."

His father regarded him. "You mean you and Dylan are going to kill someone."

Leroux's eyes bulged and he held a finger up to his lips as he closed the door. "Who the hell told you that?" he hissed.

"Your mother."

"Over the phone?"

"How else?"

Leroux closed his eyes for a moment, shaking his head. "You do realize what I do for a living, don't you? How classified everything is?"

His father stared at him. "I'm not an idiot."

"Then don't talk about this kind of stuff over the phone. You have no idea who might be listening."

"Why would they listen in on your mother and me?"

"Because of who I am."

His father frowned. "Do you really think they'd do that?"

"I work for the CIA. My girlfriend is an operative. My best friend is an operative. My best friend's girlfriend is—was, a Chinese exile. I guarantee you, somebody somewhere is listening in at least occasionally."

"Then I guess your mother and I better stop having all that phone sex."

Leroux felt a little sick. "Oh God, Dad, please!"

His father roared with laughter. "You should see your face. What, did you think a stork dropped you through the chimney one night?"

"One can always hope."

His father became serious. "Go do what you and Dylan need to do." He nodded toward Sherrie. "We'll keep an eye on her. You go get her and your friend some justice."

JFK International Airport

New York City, New York

Kane sat in the first-class lounge, his Shaws of London insurance investigator persona leaving nothing to be desired. Unfortunately, if his cover was challenged, he was off the books, and the front company answering his calls might hang him out to dry.

It all depended on how forgiving a mood Morrison was in.

He had a sense he wouldn't be very.

His phone buzzed and he checked the secure message.

Requested package will be ready upon arrival. Details attached. Have a nice flight, Mr. Kane.

He smiled. His contact in Kuala Lumpur was the same one he dealt with in the region on many occasions, and the man wasn't one to turn down any additional side contracts.

Something very useful in his business.

Sometimes you just don't want the boss to know what you're up to.

127

After all, it could get the man in trouble when questioned in front of a congressional committee.

He checked his watch. Thirty minutes to boarding, then 22 hours to Kuala Lumpur. He smiled. By this time tomorrow, one of those responsible would be dead, but not before he gave up the location of the others. He closed his eyes.

Don't worry, babe, I won't rest until they're all dead.

Outside Bethesda, Maryland

Tommy Granger sat in his old beater, a Honda Civic that had served him well for many years, and the previous owner many years before that. He had never owned a new car, not even one that still had some warranty left on it when he bought it.

That meant every one of the ever-increasing repairs came out of his pocket, though at least Mai was helping since they both drove it now.

A new car!

The very idea had his heart pounding. Yes, a lot of his generation had no desire to own a car, and many didn't even have a driver's license, but that didn't work in the world outside of the big cities. Ridesharing wasn't everywhere, mass transit was a pain in the ass, and freedom was still king.

He wanted to go where he wanted, when he wanted, without being reliant on some schedule set at city hall, or by the availability of an unknown driver and the whims of surge pricing. No, he wanted a car, and always would until some bureaucrat forced him out of it.

I'll give you my car when you pry it off my cold dead ass.

And the key to getting that new car could be this job he was about to start. It might last a day, it might last a month, he had no idea, but with what he was paid hourly last time, even just a couple of days would give them enough to top up the down payment so their regular payments would be low enough that if either of them lost their jobs, they wouldn't lose the car.

His phone vibrated and he read the message, a reply to the one he had sent moments ago when he arrived.

Sit tight.

His chest fluttered at the fear he suddenly felt.

It was awesome.

The past hour had been a rollercoaster of anxiety and excitement, and he was so on edge, Six Flags wouldn't be getting its regular customer next weekend. This was better than any video game, and though it could be dangerous, he wasn't truly scared. This was America. He was more likely to get shot going to the corner store than killed by some foreign agent.

Since his first contract with Leroux, he had been wondering what it would take to get into the CIA. Not as some spy, but an analyst. A data jockey sitting in a secure facility with no risk to him or Mai. Just a solid, steady job, decent pay and benefits, and an interesting career where his abilities as a hacker would be appreciated rather than frowned upon.

Yet something else had entered the picture over the past year, especially the past month, that had changed everything. A steady job at the CIA was cool and all, but his podcast was growing at an insane rate, especially since the incident in the Philippines. He had never really known what would happen with his life, though now that he had choices, he was torn. All he knew was that for the first time, he wanted stability. He wanted to spend his life with Mai, settle down, get married, start a family. Not right yet, but in time.

Life was good.

He had excitement in his life thanks to Professors Acton and Palmer, money coming in thanks to his podcast's advertising share, and a life he could never have imagined after his arrest as a teen for hacking the DoD mainframe.

He frowned.

And unfortunately thanks to Google, any job you apply for means your name is flagged.

He had figured he'd be forced into a life of minimum wage jobs, so instead had thrown himself into academics. And thank God he had. It was where he met Mai, the professors, and through them Chris Leroux, who had made him an unofficial spy.

I love my life!

Leroux pulled into the parking lot and stopped beside him. Tommy climbed out then into Leroux's vehicle, exchanging pleasantries.

"We're waiting for one more."

"Who?"

"Sonya."

"Oh, the hot Asian chick?"

Leroux gave him a look. "I'm sure she'd prefer to be labeled 'competent woman.'"

"Yeah, right. Sorry."

"Don't apologize to me, apologize to her."

Tommy's eyes bulged. "Do I have to? She'll know what I said!"

Leroux chuckled. "Let's keep it between the two of us. Besides, I thought you were living with a 'hot Asian chick.'"

Tommy beamed, memories of the five-minute quickie he had with Mai an hour ago sending a surge through parts unknown. "I am."

"How are things going there?"

"Excellent. I think I'm going to ask her to marry me."

Leroux smiled. "Congrats!"

Tommy's eyes widened. "Oh, not right yet. It's too soon. But I think she's the one."

Leroux became somber. "Well, all I can say is don't put off until tomorrow what you can do today. Especially with the people you love. You never know what's going to happen in life, and it might just throw you a curveball that wrecks all your plans."

Tommy stared at him. "Did something happen?"

A tear escaped Leroux's eye and it was quickly wiped away. "It's the reason we're here today. Sonya's been in the loop, so I'll brief you now. Two weeks ago, Special Agent Kane's girlfriend, Lee Fang, a former Chinese Special Forces operative who was living in exile here, was kidnapped. During the attempt, my girlfriend, Agent Sherrie White, intervened. Both were taken. Agent White was found badly beaten and is still in a coma, but Lee Fang was found dead, her body burned. We had to use DNA to confirm her identity."

Another tear was wiped away. Tommy's.

"Who-who did it?"

"The Chinese. We're assuming the government, though it could have been some rogue operation. We believe the former, as it was too well coordinated."

Tommy's sense of security slipped away. "And what are we doing here today?"

"We found one of them in Kuala Lumpur. Dylan is on his way there now, and we're going to help him find the man, then deal with any intel he might garner before…"

Tommy tensed, already fearing the answer. "Before?"

"Before he's eliminated."

"But why are *we* here today? Shouldn't the CIA be taking care of this?"

"The White House doesn't want to provoke the Chinese. They're so damned concerned with the trade ramifications of everything, that they're willing to let those bastards assault our agents and kill our assets, on our own soil." Leroux punched the steering wheel, the horn chirping. He drew a deep breath, calming himself.

"So, this is a revenge mission?"

Leroux shook his head. "It's a justice mission. We're going to find and eliminate everyone involved."

"Why?"

Leroux stared at him. "What do you mean?"

Tommy shifted in his seat, regretting his question. "I mean, it won't bring them back, and you're going to have to live with the knowledge you killed people."

"I kill people almost every day. This will be no different."

Another car pulled into the lonely parking lot.

"That's Sonya." Leroux handed him a hood. "You know the drill."

Director Morrison's Office, CIA Headquarters
Langley, Virginia

Morrison squeezed the bridge of his nose, closing his burning eyes. He had never imagined when he joined the Agency over thirty years ago that he'd spend most of his time behind a desk or in meetings, staring at screens of varying sizes all day.

The human body was never meant for it.

When he was younger, he had been a man of action, but after those fateful days in Moscow near the end of the Cold War, his spy career had been cut short.

Now he played a constant game of chess, attempting to outthink his opponents by several moves, trying to prevent wars that might be eventually lost should his adversaries gain the upper hand.

Too often with one hand tied behind his back, as it usually was when dealing with China or Russia.

Especially China.

They were simply too powerful now, and the world was too reliant upon their ability to produce goods for Western consumption at cheap prices.

Not hard when you have no labor or environmental laws hampering you.

With Russia it was different. Only the Europeans were reliant upon them, and for only one thing. Natural gas to heat their homes in the winters. Other than that, little depended upon the Russian economy, so action could be taken.

But China?

Never.

Not without significant pain.

His computer beeped indicating a secure message from outside the agency. He opened it.

Dylan Kane just boarded flight QR702 at JFK, final destination Kuala Lumpur. Do we intercept?

Morrison sighed.

So predictable.

Kuala Lumpur International Airport

Kuala Lumpur, Malaysia

Kane spotted someone paying a little bit too much attention to him out of the corner of his eye as he headed for the taxi stand outside. His flights had been uneventful, including his clearing of customs, which wasn't a surprise. It helped that he was in all the systems as a frequent business traveler, was impeccably dressed, and good looking.

It always helped.

Because society wasn't fair.

Especially outside the Western world.

Though it wasn't his job to change it, just to prevent it from infecting his own country.

His luggage was loaded into the back of a cab, and moments later, they were on their way downtown toward his hotel, booked through one of his contacts when the plane ticket was bought. He was pleased that Morrison hadn't cut him off at the knees so far. It would have been easy for him to invalidate his passport, or red flag him with Interpol. But he hadn't.

Though perhaps he had put a tail on him.

He tapped the left arm of his sunglasses, activating a rear-facing camera and watched as his tail jumped into another cab that quickly pulled from the curb.

Kane frowned. The only people who should know he was here were people he trusted implicitly. He had no doubt Morrison had people monitoring his cover, so the moment his flight was booked, or at worst the moment he checked in with his passport, Morrison had been notified. He was technically rogue on this mission, so a tail was definitely possible, however he couldn't dismiss the possibility that the very people he was after had someone on the inside.

Time and again, the Chinese were found to have moles inside pretty much every government organization, and he couldn't take that chance.

He would have to lose him, or kill him.

He was hesitant to do the latter, as they could be innocent—he wasn't about to kill a CIA operative simply doing his job.

And if the Chinese knew he was here, then they were fully aware of who he was, and would be on the lookout, his cover blown.

He spotted a café ahead and pointed. "Pull over here."

"But, sir, this isn't your hotel."

"Just pull over. I'll be about five minutes."

The cabby complied and Kane climbed out, entering the café and walking through to the back. He pretended to be checking his messages on his phone while keeping the back of his head facing the front of the small restaurant. It didn't take long before someone came through the front entrance, slowly scanning the patrons before his eyes settled on Kane's back.

The man approached and Kane prepared himself, his hand reaching for his holstered weapon before he remembered he had none. He cursed. To himself. Then breathed a sigh of relief when the man removed his sunglasses.

Kane turned to face his tail. "Hey, Jack, what the hell are you doing here?"

Jack—just Jack—shrugged. "I hear they have good coffee."

Kane chuckled. "Funny, I heard the same thing." He eyed him suspiciously. "Who sent you?"

"A little birdie at the agency."

Kane pressed. "Who?"

"I'm afraid I don't know. And that's the truth. I just got orders to follow you and watch your back. I figured it would just be easier if I let you spot me. That way you could decide how you wanted to handle things." Jack regarded him. "So, how *do* you want to handle things?"

Kane frowned. "I can't let you get involved. This is off the books, and it's going to get messy."

Jack smiled. "I like messy. It's my favorite way to do things."

Kane grunted. "Your funeral. I'm going to my hotel now. I assume you know where that is."

"Amazingly enough."

"Okay, be there in half an hour. And remember what I said. This is going to get very messy. If you're not there in thirty, I'll understand."

"Oh, I'll be there." Jack paused. "I heard what happened. I'm sorry."

A surge of emotions washed over Kane, and tears threatened to flow. He focused on the burn in his stomach as it raged over what had happened to the woman he loved. But today was not a day for mourning. Today was a day for revenge. Today was a day to punish.

And he prayed for Jack's sake the man wasn't here to interfere with the retribution about to be handed down.

Off-the-books Operations Center

Outside Bethesda, Maryland

Leroux watched Tommy and Tong manipulate the camera feeds as they monitored Kane's arrival in Kuala Lumpur. They had spent the past day firing up all the equipment, tapping whatever feeds they could, and tracking the past 24 hours of movement by their target.

The three of them had worked together in Kane's secret facility before, and they were all familiar with the gear. Over the years, Kane's lack of willingness to trust the system he worked for had him setting up his own communications network in case he was ever hung out to dry. It had proven useful on many occasions, but it wasn't until Kane had recently revealed this particular setup that Leroux realized just how paranoid Kane actually was.

What he had created was state of the art, and wasn't just an operations center. Several large shipping containers had been joined together, and they included enough supplies to last months, sleeping facilities, a bathroom, kitchen—all the comforts of home.

It was an impressive setup, and sometimes Leroux wondered just where Kane got the money to create such a facility.

Some questions are better left unasked.

"Has he arrived yet?"

Tong nodded. "Yes. He's been on the ground a little over half an hour."

"Any trouble?"

"Not that I can see."

Tommy pointed at one of the screens showing the taxi stand. "There he is."

Leroux watched as Kane climbed into the taxi and pulled away from the airport. Tommy was about to change the feed when Leroux stopped him. "Wait. Is that someone following him?"

Tommy squinted. "Where?"

Leroux pointed at another cab pulling away from the curb. "Back that up. Get me a shot of the guy that got in."

Tommy complied, and moments later he had a face. Tong mapped the facial recognition points. "Running him now." The system beeped and Tong frowned. "He's flagged."

"What does that mean?" asked Tommy.

"The code suggests he's one of ours."

"CIA?"

"Possibly. Could be special ops within DoD."

Tommy looked at both of them. "Is that good or bad?"

Leroux chewed his cheek. "It all depends on who sent him. Do we have anything in the file?"

"Just a name," replied Tong. "Jack."

Leroux's eyes narrowed. "Jack? Nothing else?"

She shook her head. "Nope. Just Jack."

"Wait a minute!" Tommy adjusted the image slightly, improving the quality, then smiled. "I know him! He's the guy that saved our asses in Mongolia!"

Leroux and Tong exchanged smiles, having been involved in the operation from a safe distance—Langley.

"This is good news, isn't it?" asked Tommy. "I mean, he's one of the good guys, isn't he? If it wasn't for him, Mai and I would be dead."

Leroux sat in his chair, scratching his chin. "Possibly. It all depends on who sent him, and what his orders are."

Tong regarded him. "Should we warn Kane?"

"Send him a secure message to his watch, though I have a funny feeling he already knows."

Grand Hyatt Kuala Lumpur
Kuala Lumpur, Malaysia

Kane sorted through the equipment his contact had left under his bed, finding everything exactly as he had expected. He had received a message from his team back home warning him about Jack just after they had parted ways, but was happy to know they had his back. Now it was a matter of waiting for them to do their real job.

Find his target.

All they knew was that the man had arrived there yesterday with three others. They had no idea where he had gone, nor why they were here. He had every faith in his team's ability to find the man again. He just hoped he could take him alive. This was their first lead in over two weeks, and he needed to get the man to talk. Ten people had been involved on the ground. Three had been killed by Sherrie and Fang, which meant seven remained alive.

He wanted all of them dead.

Yet they were merely foot soldiers. They had to be following orders from someone. And that someone was his ultimate goal.

A knock at the door had him grabbing a Glock from the bed. He peered through the peephole and found Jack grinning at him. Kane shook his head and opened the door, letting the operative inside. He checked his watch. "Thirty minutes, right on time."

Jack smiled. "I know, I'm good, right?"

"You're punctual." Kane returned to checking his equipment. "I assume the fact you're here means you're in."

"Was there ever any doubt?"

"After the insanity you pulled in Mongolia, I guess not."

"Don't worry, I'm in one-hundred-percent. You don't screw around with friends or family." Jack surveyed the equipment lying on the bed. "You planning on starting a war?"

"Only a small one, and only if I have to."

"So, just who are we going after?"

"A man named Han Zhanshu. He's linked with the Chinese foreign service. He was part of the hit team that took out Fang and almost took out Sherrie."

"Who do you think is behind this?"

Kane glanced at him. "Do you know who Fang really was?"

"Not a clue."

"She was former Chinese Special Forces. She helped us during that coup attempt a couple of years back."

"So, you think the Chinese have been looking for her all this time and finally found her?"

Kane shook his head and took a seat. "I don't know. If they had really wanted to find her, they could have quite easily. She kept a fairly low profile, but it wasn't like she was in hiding. The sophistication of the operation they just executed was impressive. They were able to tap into pretty much any camera feed they wanted to. If they have that capability, I think they would have been monitoring camera feeds all over the country looking for her. The Chinese have sophisticated facial recognition software that could do the job. I have a feeling they knew exactly where she was all along. I think they just decided to leave her where she was as long as she kept her mouth shut."

"Why? What does she know?"

"She knows who was involved on the Chinese side of the coup attempt. She even killed one of the generals involved. Yee Wei."

Jack fetched a bottle of water from the minibar and held it up. Kane nodded and the bottle was tossed then another one grabbed. "You think it was a revenge thing? Somebody finally gained enough power to have Daddy avenged?"

"Possible. There have been some changes in the command structure there recently. The hardliners have been firming up control."

"Could one of those generals she has information on be in play right now? Maybe he wanted to eliminate anyone that might have dirt on him?"

Kane chewed his cheek for a moment as he thought. It was a possibility. International laws didn't apply to the Chinese. They were too powerful now. They knew they could never be challenged militarily. The governments of the West had been blinded in their attempts to gain access to a market of 1.4 billion people, as well as a cheap labor force. Greed had created an economic and military powerhouse that had no interest in playing by the rules the rest of the world abided by. It was too late to stop them. The Chinese had already won, the West just didn't know it yet—or weren't willing to admit it.

The Chinese could take Taiwan tomorrow and all America could do was protest. Nobody was willing to go to war anymore for countries that meant nothing to them. Afghanistan was revenge, Iraq was oil and politics, ISIS was self-preservation. But Taiwan? Hong Kong? Hell, there were dozens of countries at risk in the region including the Philippines, Pakistan, India, and more. And as the Chinese military's capabilities continued to rapidly progress, they grew increasingly invulnerable. And once their blue water naval capabilities gave them the capacity to wield their influence on the seas, there would be nothing that anyone could do.

It had been a race.

The hope had been that the middle class within China would grow rapidly, and by giving them access to Western culture and values, they would demand democracy of their government. What the West hadn't counted on, was the rapid progression of technology that had allowed the Chinese to limit outside information from reaching its people. The dystopian state depicted in so many movies and novels already existed here on Earth today.

It was the Chinese surveillance state.

Millions of cameras tied into central databases with instant facial recognition software capable of identifying and tracking anyone at any time meant dissent inside the borders was nearly impossible. The proof they had already brainwashed their citizenry was the reaction of the Chinese population to the protests in Hong Kong.

And then the proof that the Chinese government's influence extended to their diaspora outside their borders could be seen in the protests taking place in America, Canada, and other nations in support of the Hong Kong government, as opposed to those demanding democracy.

China's power within its borders was absolute, and extended across the globe with its emigrants. So, it would be within character for the government to reach out and kill Fang if they now perceived her as some sort of threat.

Even on American soil.

Kane finally looked at Jack. "You could be right."

"So, what do you want to do about it?"

"Let's take it one step at a time. Let's find this guy, see what he knows, then move on to the next."

"Are you going to let him live?"

"Not a chance in hell."

Off-the-books Operations Center

Outside Bethesda, Maryland

"I've got him." Tong pointed at the screen and Leroux smiled. Their target, Han Zhanshu, could be seen exiting the airport in Kuala Lumpur with three others. The three didn't match any of the seven they were seeking, though might be connected to the operation from two weeks ago in other ways.

"We need to know where they went."

"Already on it. One nice thing about Kuala Lumpur is lots of traffic cameras to tap."

Leroux watched as Tong expertly manipulated the feeds Tommy had hacked, tracking the van that had picked up their four suspects. It wasn't long before they had a final destination for them.

The Chinese Embassy.

"Good work. Now run forward on any cameras showing the exits of that compound. Let's see if they ever left."

Tommy glanced over his shoulder at Leroux. "What if they didn't? Kane doesn't think he can break into a Chinese embassy, does he?"

"Breaking in is easy. It's getting out alive that's the hard part."

Outside the Chinese Embassy
Kuala Lumpur, Malaysia

Kane and Jack sat in their car just down the street from the Chinese Embassy. A review of the tapes suggested their target had never left the compound after he had arrived, though it was a distinct possibility he had left in a vehicle with tinted windows or in a hidden compartment.

Anything was possible, though there was one reason for optimism.

There had been no reports of the disappearance or murder of any former Chinese nationals in Malaysia over the past 24 hours.

It suggested he was still in the country, awaiting final orders, or for the opportunity to execute his current assignment with his three buddies.

The easiest way to take him would be outside of the embassy, but they didn't have time to wait.

"Are you sure you don't want me to take the shot?"

Kane glanced over his shoulder at Jack. "I'm sure."

"I'm a very good shot."

"Believe it or not, so am I. That's why we're both super-secret agents."

"I'm superer though. I only have one name."

Kane grunted. "That's an affectation, not a qualification. Just because you never want to tell any of us your last name doesn't mean you don't have one."

"I'm 'the man with one name.'" He delivered it in a Clint Eastwood voice that wasn't too bad an approximation.

"You do know he was the man with *no* name, and that he never actually called himself that."

"True, but wouldn't it have been cool if he did? You'd have him and the bad guy squaring off, and some kid would tug on a bystander's sleeve and ask, who's he fighting, mister? And the man would reply, the man with no name. Yeah, what's his name? The man with no name. Yeah, him. What's his name? I dawgawned told ya twice, yungun', the man with no name!"

Kane shook his head. "You're a little touched, aren't you? Maybe you just can't remember your last name. Ever thought of that?"

Jack shrugged. "As good an explanation as any. Now, are you going to take that shot or what?"

"I was waiting for you to shut up."

"If past experience is any indication, you could be waiting a while."

Kane squeezed the trigger, propelling the jamming device across the road and onto the metal pole in the corner of the compound holding one of the security cameras. "Bullseye."

Jack slapped him on the back. "I knew you had it in you."

Kane ignored him, instead activating his comms. "You guys ready?"

"Affirmative. On your mark."

"Good. Stand by." Kane stepped out of the car and casually strolled across the street, tapping his phone to activate the jammer. He quickly scaled the wall, flipping over the top, then dropped to the ground on the other side, rushing toward the large diesel generator. He unscrewed the fuel cap then reached into his pocket, dropping several capsules inside, then returned to the car, deactivating the jammer the moment he was inside.

"That was rather boring."

Kane grunted. "Sometimes boring is good." He activated his comms. "Control, proceed."

"Stand by."

After a few seconds, the lights went out, bathing the entire area in darkness. A moment later, the diesel generator roared to life, the compound awash in light once again.

"Good job. How much of the city did you take out?" asked Kane.

"Just that block I hope," replied Leroux. "Why? Are you seeing something we aren't?"

"Well, it looks like the whole damned city went out from where we're sitting."

"Are you serious?"

Kane laughed at the panic in his friend's voice. "No."

Jack grinned, punching Kane on the shoulder. "You're evil."

Kane shrugged. "Sorry, buddy, had to do it. Everything looks good here. Stand by."

The generator's engine continued to roar with a growing intensity as the capsules kicked in, triggering diesel engine runaway.

"How long do those things take?" asked Jack.

"Not long. Sounds like they're about—"

The diesel generator erupted into a fireball, shooting flames and black smoke into the air as the windows of the surrounding buildings rattled. Screams erupted from some spooked neighbors, and the few on the streets at this time of night bolted.

The embassy gates opened as staff poured out along with security, seeking safety off the compound. There were perhaps a few dozen, the embassy quiet at this hour.

Jack pointed. "There's our guy."

Kane sneered, his heart pounding as he reached for his weapon. Jack placed a steadying hand on his forearm.

"Remember why we're here."

Kane sighed. "Let's do this."

"Wait. His buddies just joined him."

"We're prepared for that." Kane put the car in gear and slowly drove toward the gate. The four they were interested in were huddled together at the far end of the sidewalk, exactly as he would expect from people who weren't part of the regular contingent. Jack lit a set of firecrackers then tossed them over the wall, their rattle moments later sending the staff into an even more intense panic, and the guards rushing back through the gate to investigate.

"Now."

Kane gave the car some more gas, not enough to draw any attention with an over-revving engine, then came to a stop in front of the four men. He stepped out, drawing two tasers, deploying them into the two men on the left, Jack doing the same from the passenger seat to the two on the right. All four dropped, writhing in agony, and Kane kept the voltage flowing as he rounded the hood of the car and grabbed his target. Jack held open the rear door and Kane tossed the man inside. Jack zip-tied the man's hands and feet as Kane climbed back into the driver's seat then hammered on the gas, sending them surging down the roadway. One quick turn and they were out of sight.

"Control, tell me you still have the traffic cameras disabled."

"Confirmed. Let us know when you're clear."

Kane took a couple more turns then drove behind a large industrial plant, the area abandoned. "We're clear."

"Restoring power. Stand by."

Kane watched the lights turn back on in the rearview mirror. "Any sign of activity at the embassy?"

"Lots of confused faces but no signs of pursuit. It looks like you got away clean."

Kane smiled. "Good. Stand by while we start the interrogation."

There was a pause at Leroux's end. "It's not too late to back out."

Kane stared in the rearview mirror at their prisoner. "Do you really want me to?"

Another pause. "No."

"Good. You might not want to listen in. Especially Tommy."

"Understood. I'll monitor, no one else."

Kane frowned. "Perhaps Sonya—"

"No. I'll do it. This is our op, not theirs. They shouldn't have to hear what's about to happen. This is on my conscience, not theirs."

Kane opened his door. "It's on both of ours."

Off-the-books Operations Center
Outside Bethesda, Maryland

Tommy stared at Leroux and removed his headset. "Why can't we listen in?"

Tong shook her head. "You're not ready for something like that."

Tommy eyed her. "Why? They're just going to interrogate the guy, right? What's the big deal? Smack him around a little, waterboard him, whatever it is they do these days. I can take it. I watch movies."

Leroux sat and stared at him. "I don't think you realize what's about to happen. And movies never prepare you for anything, not when you helped put that human being into harm's way."

Tommy paled slightly. "This guy is guilty, right? I mean, we didn't just—"

Leroux nodded. "Yes, he's guilty. Absolutely guilty. He helped kill Fang, he helped beat Sherrie nearly to death. He's guilty, and we hope he's going to lead us to the others. But he's still a human being who's about to go through something unimaginable, then die tonight after he tells us what we want. And the three of us had a hand in it."

Sweat beaded on Tommy's forehead. "I-I thought we were just helping watch Kane's back. I-I didn't really think…"

Leroux reached forward and squeezed Tommy's shoulder. "I know, and I'm sorry. I should have made it clearer." Leroux leaned back, giving Tommy some space. "If you want to leave, I'll understand. In fact, I think you should leave. I never should have asked you to—"

Tommy held up a hand, cutting Leroux off. "No." He drew a deep breath. "From what I understand, these people will never see justice because of who they are."

"Correct."

"And the only way they can ever be punished for what they did is if we all help Kane."

"Yes."

Tommy squeezed his eyes shut for a moment, drawing a slow, steady breath, his mind racing with the implications of what he had been drawn into. This was real life, not a movie. People would die, and by staying, he was helping kill them. He might not be pulling the trigger, but he was helping find the targets, and guiding Kane to them.

It's like you're operating a drone. The drone might have fired the missile, but it never would have if you didn't pull the trigger.

His mouth watered and he swallowed. What was almost a game a moment ago was now a harsh reality. But they were on the side of right. These were bad people who had done a bad thing. And if this was the only way for Fang and Sherrie to get some justice for what had happened to them, then who was he to say it wasn't right? If he left now, he'd be replaced within hours, and whatever was about to happen would still happen regardless. But the delay replacing him might allow the next target to escape.

And he couldn't live with himself if his actions allowed that to occur.

He looked at Tong then at Leroux. "You need me. The two of you can't do this by yourselves. This is a three-person job, just like last time. I'm staying."

Leroux peered into his eyes, as if seeking the truth. "Are you sure?"

Tommy shrugged. "Not in the least, but I'm going to stay regardless."

Leroux smiled. "Good man. You remind me of myself a few years ago. I was scared shitless too, but I did it. You'll do fine. Just remember that the people we're dealing with are guilty of unspeakable crimes, crimes that go far beyond just Fang and Sherrie."

Tommy drew a quick breath of courage. "Then let's kick some ass!"

Tong laughed then Leroux became serious, pressing his headset against his ear. "It's started."

Suddenly Tommy wasn't so sure he had made the right decision, his stomach flipping and bile filling his mouth.

I wonder if my imagination is worse than the real thing.

He heard a scream from Leroux's earpiece, the man, not much older than him, staring directly ahead, his face devoid of emotion. As if he'd heard this a thousand times before. Tommy shuddered.

What kind of life is that?

The question had him reconsidering his desire to work for the CIA.

Kuala Lumpur, Malaysia

Kane stepped back, giving his fists a rest. Their target, Han Zhanshu, was tied to a lamppost, the light overhead shot out by Jack, giving them some additional privacy in the empty parking lot. Han had been tenderized for the past fifteen minutes, questions shouted at him by Jack as Kane delivered a beating to the body, neither expecting any answers at first.

Han was a trained Chinese operative. He'd have been taught pain management techniques, but those only lasted so long, even the strongest eventually breaking. He had avoided the face for the most part, not wanting to risk the man's brain despite the overwhelming desire to deliver a beating that matched the intensity of the one dealt to Sherrie.

But he had a purpose here, and an equitable beating wasn't it.

He held the man's drooping head up and stared him in the eyes. "Ready to talk?" he asked in perfect Chinese.

"Go to hell, American," replied the man in equally perfect English.

Kane smiled. "So, you speak English. Good. Ready to talk?"

"I said go to hell."

"You first." Kane delivered a flurry of blows to the man's chest and stomach, the distinct sound of a breaking rib and an agonizing gasp confirming a new painful injury. He stepped back and motioned to Jack. "Show him the first photo."

Jack held it up. "Recognize him?"

"I'm not telling you anything."

Kane jabbed a taser into Han's side, sending 50,000 volts through his prisoner's body. "I won't waste your time. Of course you recognize him. You were on an op together in Virginia two weeks ago. You and nine others. You killed Lee Fang, and seriously beat a friend of mine."

Han slumped, only his bonds holding him in place. "I don't know what you're talking about."

Kane tased him again, then pressed the barrel of his Glock against the man's balls. "Would you like me to shoot off the left one, or the right? I live in a democracy, so I'm giving you a choice."

Han raised his head and stared at Kane, his energy sapped, his words slightly slurred. "Go ahead. We both know you're going to kill me."

Kane stepped back with a smile and flourish. "Ahh, but the question is *how* I'm going to kill you. I have until morning, then I have a flight to catch. Now, I'd like to have a nice night's sleep before I get on that plane, but it's business class, so I guess I could sleep on the flight. It's all really up to you. Do you want me to get *on* the flight well-rested, having killed you quickly and painlessly, or do you want me to arrive at my destination, still well-rested, having killed you slowly over the next eight hours?" He tased him again, this time in the nuts, a flood of urine his reward. "What would you prefer?"

Off-the-books Operations Center
Outside Bethesda, Maryland

Leroux kept the emotions off his face as best he could. What was happening had happened before, though it was rare. It was technically illegal, though it was a gray area for CIA operatives on foreign soil of a non-ally.

Illegal or not, it didn't make it any easier to listen to.

He pictured Sherrie, and what she must have gone through, and drew strength from it. Had this man shown her any mercy? Had they shown Fang any mercy? They had no idea what kind of beating had been delivered to her. The remains were so badly burned, little had been left to perform an autopsy on.

And now he was listening to one of those responsible suffering a beating equally as harsh.

It made him warm inside.

"Sir, something's happening at the consulate."

Leroux stepped over to Tong's station. "What?"

Tong pointed at one of the displays. He leaned in to see footage from a camera planted across the street earlier by Kane. Two vehicles were emerging from inside the gates in a hurry, turning in the direction Kane and Jack had left with their target.

"Do you think they know where they went?" asked Tommy.

Leroux shook his head. "No." He paused. "Unless the guy has a tracker on him." He cursed, activating his comms. "Arrow, Control. Two vehicles just left the consulate. They might be headed your way. Your target may have a tracker on him, over."

"Copy that. ETA?"

Leroux glanced at the map. "Five minutes."

"Copy that. Let me know when they're two minutes out."

Kuala Lumpur, Malaysia

Han Zhanshu had gained Kane's respect. To a point. The level of pain the man had gone through over the past half-hour was phenomenal, and he hadn't broken. Kane lifted the man's chin, knowing time was running out.

A different tactic had to be tried.

"You have a tracker, don't you?"

The man's eyes drifted up for a moment before sagging. A slight smile emerged.

"That's why you've been hanging on. You thought they would come and save you. Unfortunately for you, I know they're on their way, and my people will give us plenty of warning before they get here. You're going to die in about three minutes." Kane lifted Han's chin, lowering his voice. "Don't worry, I'm done torturing you. It will be a clean kill." He held up the photos again. "You've told me nothing, but I found you, and I'll find the others eventually. But tell me this. Three of your men died on that mission. Don't you think the person responsible deserves to die as well? Which of these men do you hold responsible?"

Han stared at Kane, saying nothing for a moment, then finally gave in, his entire body sagging. "Wang Keqiang."

Kane quickly flipped to Wang's photo, holding it up. "Him?"

Han nodded.

"Where can I find him?"

"Macao. City of Dreams Casino."

Leroux's voice interrupted in Kane's ear. "Two minutes."

"Copy that." Kane lifted Han's sagging head. "Thanks." He drew his weapon and put two through Han's skull.

Off-the-books Operations Center

Outside Bethesda, Maryland

Leroux watched the satellite tracking as Kane and Jack left the area before the Chinese security detail could arrive. All they would find was their dead comrade and a bunch of unanswered questions. He checked the time. "Book them on the first flight out of there that will get them to Macao."

Tong nodded. "On it."

"And Tommy, monitor all communications for any mention of what just happened. Anything with Kane or Jack's description, anything that suggests the authorities might be looking for them."

Tommy, still shaken by what he was now involved in, exhaled loudly. "Yes, sir."

We might have to arrange some counseling for him when this is all done.

Granger/Trinh Residence

St. Paul, Maryland

Tommy stared at himself in the mirror. Leroux had sent him home to decompress and get some proper rest while they waited for Kane's plane to arrive in Macao. Tong was holding down the fort while Leroux checked on Sherrie. It wasn't much time, only about five hours, but it was appreciated.

And needed.

He had spent almost half an hour in the shower silently crying, picturing what had happened to the man in Malaysia before he was shot. His mind was filling in the blanks of what Kane had done to the man, and no matter how bad he was, Tommy was having trouble processing the actions of the so-called good guys.

A few hours' sleep in his own bed with Mai holding him had him fairly refreshed, though still troubled. As he buttoned his shirt, Mai brought him a bowl of his favorite morning starter—oatmeal with fresh fruit. He gave her a weak smile then ate several spoonsful while leaning against the dresser. And it had no appeal. He put it down.

"Not hungry?"

"Not really." His shoulders shook and the tears flowed the moment Mai took him in her arms. "I-I'm sorry. I don't know why I keep crying."

"It's okay, don't apologize. Why don't you tell me what happened?"

"I-I can't. I don't want you to know what I did."

Mai pushed back from him slightly, staring up at him. "What could you have possibly done that you wouldn't want to tell me? It's not like you were off killing somebody."

He gasped out another cry and lay back on the bed, curling into a ball. Mai sat beside him, gently stroking his head.

"Tell me, please. I can take it."

"I-I killed somebody last night."

The stroking stopped, though only for a moment. "I find that hard to believe. Why don't you tell me *exactly* what happened?"

"We were running what they call an op, I guess. Kane and another agent were in Malaysia. They kidnapped this bad guy, tortured him, then killed him."

Mai's eyes widened. "That's terrible!" She regained control. "But I'm sure he deserved it, right?"

Tommy sniffed, wiping away his tears. "Yes. He was bad. Really bad. He was one of the ones who killed Fang and beat Sherrie."

"And what makes you think *you* killed him?"

"Well, I helped find him. If I hadn't found him, then he'd still be alive."

"Which means the bad guy would have gotten away with murder."

Another sniff. "I suppose."

"And by that logic, everyone involved in the arrest of a murderer who is then executed, is guilty of murder as well. You know that makes no sense. If this man hadn't done what he had, he'd be alive today. You should be proud you helped bring someone to justice."

Tommy drew a deep breath and held it for several seconds before letting the air escape with a gasp. "You're right, I guess. It's just the way it happened. I mean, Leroux and Tong. They just sat there while it happened. No emotions. Nothing. It was as if they do this every day. Actually, I think that's what Leroux said. That he killed people almost every day." He shook his head. "I don't think the CIA is for me."

Mai smiled, squeezing the back of his neck as she leaned in and gave him a kiss. "Neither do I. Listen, you should tell them you can't do this. You have no obligation to go back."

Tommy shook his head. "No, they need my help. And these *are* bad people. They deserve to die."

"That may be true, but not everyone is cut out for this line of work."

"May-maybe I'll get used to it."

She frowned. "I hope you never do."

Tommy's eyes went wide. "Why would you say something like that?"

"Because I don't know if I want to be with someone who can get used to helping kill someone."

He stared at her for a moment. "So, if I were a soldier, and was sent to war, you couldn't love me?"

She stared at him, aghast. "That's not at all what I meant!"

"Well, it's the same thing."

"How is it?"

"This is war. The Chinese came to our country, killed someone who lives here, and nearly killed one of our citizens, one of our people who fight to keep people like you and me safe. If that's not war, I don't know what is."

She smiled, patting his cheek. "And now that you've said that, how do you feel about what you did?"

He stared at her then smiled. "You just played me, didn't you?"

She shrugged. "Maybe. Maybe not." She winked, then became serious. "Just remember, don't lose who you are in this. I mean, you're *so* sensitive. And I don't mean that in a bad way!" she hurriedly added. "I mean, you have a lot of compassion in you, empathy. You're the most empathetic guy I know."

Tommy sat up in the bed, grabbing a tissue. "Hey, just because I cry when we watch Notting Hill doesn't mean I'm a, well, you know…"

"Hopeless romantic?"

He smiled slightly. "Is it that obvious?"

"Yes, and I love you for it." She placed a hand on his chest. "It's what's in here that made me fall in love with you. If you want to help this Leroux guy, then I'll support you. Just don't let what you're doing change who you are inside."

He hugged her, hard. "I promise."

He just hoped it was a promise he could keep.

City of Dreams Casino

Macao Special Administrative Region, China

Kane sat at the bar, a scotch in one hand, the other ready for action should it become necessary. They had found their target quickly enough—he wasn't exactly keeping a low profile.

And it was disturbing how much in common his old self had with this man.

This had been his life. Complete a mission, then go to a resort or casino somewhere exotic and drink himself into a stupor while enjoying fine food and fast women.

It had been a wonderfully destructive existence.

But that was no longer him. Not since Fang had entered his life.

Though now, with her gone, he feared he might return to his old ways, and with little to live for, the risks he had been willing to take before, might pale in comparison to those he might now take.

Focus on your family. On your friends. You still have something to live for.

172

He took a sip of his drink, nursing it slowly. He had to be at the top of his game. Judging by the large bets and bigger losses, their target was about to leave the table and return to his suite upstairs. He was playing the high roller, and either the Chinese paid their operatives a hell of a lot more than Uncle Sam paid him, or Wang Keqiang had been earning a little something on the side.

Just like him.

His extracurricular earnings weren't illegal, and were never as a result of the job. He didn't take bribes, he didn't steal money from drug dealers or terrorists. All those things were turned over and cataloged.

His extra funds came from this side of his life. He was well-suited to poker and other games where reading one's opponents was key. If he ever wanted funds, he could always find a high-stakes game.

Then there were the women. He had lost count of how many times he had woken the next morning to find some token of a woman's appreciation left on the nightstand as if he were a gigolo.

"Mr. Kane, so good to see you again."

Speaking of.

He turned toward the sultry voice behind him, a gorgeous socialite he had bedded a couple of times on the job—and off—over the years. "Mrs. Yang, so good to see you." He gave her the once over she always appreciated, the mid-forties woman giving him a titillating spin. "You look as lovely as ever."

Yang ran a finger down his chest. "As do you."

Kane thought of the women he'd had to sleep with on the job, and how he had come clean to Fang about how sometimes he still had to do it. It had been torturing him, but she had been fine with it, understanding that it was all part of the job.

She was the best.

Was.

"What's troubling you, my love? Is it something I can help you with?" She eyed him like the cougar she was. "Perhaps we could go back to my room and I could help you forget those troubles."

He forced a smile. "You have no idea how much I'd like that, my dear, but I have an important meeting in a few minutes."

A pout showed her disappointment. "Perhaps the next time I'm in town." She frowned. "Oh, but I don't know when I'll be here without my husband."

Kane chuckled. "If I recall correctly, the last time we were together, he was down here on the casino floor."

She leaned in. 'And we were on the floor of your suite."

She was a beautiful woman, and if she were part of the job, it wouldn't be a horrible thing, but tonight he was here for one thing only.

Revenge.

His target rose, all the chips in front of him gone.

And he didn't look at all bothered.

He headed for the elevators, a woman on each arm, the night apparently not a total loss. It never was in Macao if you had enough money. He spotted Jack making for the same elevator.

Kane checked his watch. "I'm afraid I have to go to my meeting." He kissed Mrs. Yang's hand. "Until next time."

"I can't wait."

Jack boarded the elevator and pressed the button for the floor one below the penthouse level. He stepped to the back as several others boarded. The elevator slowly made its way upward, periodically dumping its passengers, until finally it was only him, his target, and the floozies.

The man was clearly sparing no expense—penthouse suites at this casino were not cheap, nor was his arm candy.

He must have got a good bonus for killing Fang.

Jack had never met her, but understood love. And loss. It was why he avoided it at all costs. Why love someone that could leave you. Why love someone that might die before you, or, more likely in his business, would be left behind to mourn. Love wasn't for people in this business. Look what was happening to Kane. He was a tortured soul, who would likely remain that way for the rest of his life.

A life that might be shortened because of his lack of focus.

The elevator chimed and he excused himself, one of the ladies stepping aside. He felt a hand grab his ass then some giggles. He turned to find it was Wang's hand.

"Care to join us?"

Jack smiled. "Am I joining them, or you?"

Wang's hand cupped Jack's boys. "All of us."

Jack's smile spread. It wasn't the plan, but if the man was inviting him into the room, who was he to say no? "I think I'd like that."

Wang beamed. "Excellent. I think this is going to be a fabulous night, don't you girls?"

Coos of agreement were the response, including one from Kane over the small earpiece fit snugly in his ear.

"Should I give you two time to have some fun first?"

So, you want to play it that way, huh?

"I have a friend. I think you'd like him. Can he join us?"

"Bastard," muttered Kane.

Wang nodded. "The more the merrier, if he's open-minded."

Jack chuckled. "Oh, he's the most open-minded man I know. You two are going to hit it off smashingly."

Off-the-books Operations Center

Outside Bethesda, Maryland

Leroux suppressed a smile at Tommy's bug-eyed expression. He had listened to and watched so many sexual encounters over the years, nothing shocked him anymore.

Though young Tommy Granger might be about to get quite the initiation into espionage's boudoir.

"Umm, is Jack gay?"

Leroux shrugged. "How should I know?"

"But Kane, he's not, right?"

Leroux toyed with him. "I don't know. Does it matter?"

"Of course it does! They're about to have sex with that guy!"

Tong snickered. "Umm, no, they're about to kill that guy. Two minutes ago they were going to have to trick themselves into the room. Now they've been invited. It doesn't get any better than that."

Tommy's head slowly bobbed as he finally realized what was happening. Then his mouth was agape again. "But what about Jack? It's going to take time for Kane to get there."

"If I know him, he's going to take the long route." Tong grinned. "Through Cleveland."

Leroux chuckled. "The things our agents do for their country."

"Or *who* they do."

Tommy's jaw dropped. "Do these guys actually have sex on the job? I mean, like James Bond?"

Leroux nodded. "If the job calls for it."

Tommy shook his head. "Man, I think I'm rethinking this CIA thing."

Tong eyed him. "Don't you have a girlfriend?"

Tommy flushed. "Oh yeah, right. Forgot about that."

Tong patted him on the cheek. "I'm sure you'd have eventually remembered."

Tommy's eyes widened. "Don't tell her I, umm, said that."

"Your secret is safe with us." Tong pointed at the screen. "There goes Kane."

Tommy was back on the topic. "Do you think he could have had sex with that woman he was talking to?"

Leroux and Tong exchanged glances, Tong replying. "Oh yeah. Definitely."

"But what about Fang?"

"If the job demands it."

Tommy shook his head. "I shoulda been a spy."

Tong snorted. "Yeah, if only you had told your guidance counselor in school that you wanted to be a spy instead of a hacker, you'd be gallivanting around the world killing bad guys and sleeping with hot chicks while the good woman sat at home waiting for you to grace her with your presence."

Tommy stared at her, his jaw slack.

Leroux swatted the back of Tong's chair. "Give the kid a break."

Tong punched Tommy's shoulder. "I'm just messing with you. You know, haze the new guy?"

Leroux leaned in, lowering his voice. "You're lucky it's the new millennium. You wouldn't believe what they used to do to the new guy."

Tong pointed. "He's in the elevator."

Tommy leaned in, squinting. "Did he just hit the buttons for a few extra floors?"

Kane grinned at the camera he knew they were watching him on. "I just want Jack to have a chance to get comfortable."

City of Dreams Casino

Macao Special Administrative Region, China

Jack wasn't comfortable.

And he was confused.

He had two fists full of ass and a Chinese man's tongue down his throat. He was trained for this, though had to admit this was the first time he had French-kissed a man. If it weren't for the booze and cigarettes that went along with the breath, he might have been able to close his eyes and imagine something else—the man was remarkably closely shaved.

There was a knock at the door and Jack broke away. "That will be my friend. Now remember, make him feel as welcome as you did me." He opened the door and gave Kane a look out of sight of the others. "You took your sweet time," he hissed.

"I wanted you to get things warmed up." Kane tapped Jack's confused member. "Ooh, half-staff. Should I give you two a few more minutes?"

Jack grabbed him by the scruff of the neck and turned, a beaming smile on display for the others. "My friends, I'd like you to meet Dylan." He led Kane toward the party, the girls clearly thrilled to see the ruggedly handsome agent, Wang already stepping out of his pants.

"You were right, he's gorgeous."

Jack squeezed Kane's ass. "And open-minded."

Kane winked then took a martini from one of the girls, giving it a sip before placing it on the glass table occupying the space between two large couches. He reached into his pocket, pulling out his handkerchief and Jack reached into his own, doing the same.

Jack grabbed one of the girls by the waist and drew her close. "Now, we don't want to forget our lady friends, do we?" He spun her around, grinding himself into her, then placed the handkerchief over her mouth, Kane doing the same only feet away. Wang stared at them, wide-eyed, uncertain as to what was happening as the struggling girls soon fell silent.

Jack placed his gently on the couch then took the confused Wang's hand and led him toward the bedroom.

"What's going on?"

"We want you all to ourselves."

A shaky smile appeared, then Wang sashayed into the bedroom, grinning.

Kane shook his head. "The man's a fool. No wonder Han Zhanshu thought he botched the mission."

Wang stopped and turned, confusion again on his face. "Han Zhanshu. How do you know that name?"

Kane drew his weapon and pointed it at Wang. "Because last night he told me how to find you before I put two bullets in his head."

Off-the-books Operations Center

Outside Bethesda, Maryland

Leroux watched as Kane stepped back from the camera he had just set up so they could monitor what was going on.

"Got it?"

"Affirmative. We can see you now."

Wang was naked from the waist down, his hands tied to the headboard, his feet to the bedposts. Spread-eagle, he was afforded no dignity.

A common interrogation technique.

Kane sat on the bed beside the man. "Now, we're going to have a little conversation. Every time you tell me something, you get a reward. Every time you don't, you get punished. When I killed Han last night, I was in a hurry, and outside. I just caused him so much pain that in the end, he gave me your location."

Wang stared at him, terror on his face. "Yet you still killed him!"

"Yes." Kane leaned in closer. "And he knew he was going to die. He gave you up because he blamed you for the death of the three who you lost on that mission."

"What mission?"

"Oh, I'm sorry, you two have worked together before where three of your comrades died? Let me help you narrow it down. United States. Virginia. Where you killed Lee Fang."

Wang eyed him with suspicion. "Who is she to you?"

"She was the woman I loved."

Renewed fear stared back at Kane. "I was just following orders."

"I know you were. And before I kill you, you're going to tell me the locations of the other men involved in the mission that day, and the name of who gave you the orders."

Wang vigorously shook his head. "I-I can't. They'll kill me."

"No, they won't."

"What do you mean? Once they find out—"

Kane patted the man on the chest. "They won't kill you because I'm going to kill you before I leave here tonight."

"Then why should I tell you anything?"

Kane turned to Jack. "Show him the video."

Jack pulled out his phone and brought up a video he had taken of Han's final moments, showing it to Wang.

Kane pointed at the video. "See his pain? See what he went through? Wouldn't you rather avoid all that and just tell me where the others are, and who gave you the orders?"

Wang shook his head, though the terror in his eyes from the video was clear. "I'm not a traitor."

Kane smiled. "So, it *was* officially sanctioned by the Chinese government. Interesting."

Wang's eyes bulged. "I-I didn't say that!"

"If it wasn't, then you wouldn't be a traitor."

"It's...it's complicated."

"It always is." Kane drew a knife from a hidden pocket of his jacket. He slowly drew it along the delicate skin of Wang's scrotum. The man caught his breath, wincing with fear. "Left, or right?"

"What?"

"Left or right. Which should I cut out first?" Kane smiled. "You're communist, so how about we go with the left?"

Wang struggled against his bonds to no avail. "No! Please! I'll tell you anything you want, but don't do that, please! Listen, I was just following orders. Just like you do every day. I didn't kill her. That wasn't the mission. We were just sent in to grab her. I don't know what they did with her after. Please, I'll tell you everything I know, but you have to let me go. I'll give you the names and locations of the others, and I'll give you the name of the general who sent us on the mission. But you have to let me live."

Kane smiled. "You have a deal."

Tommy stared wide-eyed at the display. "That was rather easy!" He peered at a close-up of Wang's face. "Is he on drugs? He certainly seemed pretty out of it earlier."

Tong chuckled. "Well, it might be because Jack dosed his drink while he was in the casino."

Tommy's eyes widened. "Huh? How?"

"Why do you think we were listening in on the man's drink order while he was playing?"

Tommy sighed, shaking his head. "I, umm, I thought you were just being thorough."

Leroux laughed. "No, we got his order so Jack could dose it at the bar. He's on amobarbital. He'll tell us pretty much anything."

"Then why all the threats?"

"He still has to be induced to talk. Besides, Kane wants the man to feel a little fear before he kills him."

"But I thought they had a deal?"

Tong tsked at Tommy. "Oh, how much you have to learn, padawan."

City of Dreams Casino

Macao Special Administrative Region, China

Kane activated his comms, Wang's unloading of everything he knew about those involved finally finished. "Did you get all that?"

"Affirmative," replied Leroux. "We're running the intel now. Hopefully we'll get something for you shortly. I'm running that General Zhang Quanguo as well."

"Good." Kane turned to Wang. "Now, do you have anything to say before I kill you?"

Wang's jaw dropped. "But I thought we had a deal? I told you everything you wanted to know."

"Yes, you did, but I don't make deals with the men who killed the woman I loved."

"I told you! I didn't kill her! The mission was to retrieve her and bring her back to China!"

"Yet something went wrong, didn't it? You had to change your plans because someone else showed up and tried to stop you." Kane rose, drawing his weapon then screwing in the suppressor. "You nearly beat my friend to death, then you killed Fang. Your mission failed, and because of that, you killed her!" He pointed his weapon at Wang's head. "And now you're going to die. I just wish we could burn you alive like you did her!"

Wang's eyes bulged. "Wait! You don't understand, that wasn't her!"

Kane paused. "Don't try to bullshit me. We know it was her. The DNA matched."

Wang shook his head furiously. "No, you don't understand. We never killed her there. That was a decoy. We brought her back to China."

Kane wasn't certain of what to make of what was being said. Wang was clearly buying time, but for what purpose? Did the man really think they were that stupid? "Do you think we're fools? At least die with some dignity, not spewing ridiculous lies."

"No! No! You don't understand. When we arrived in China, she was handed over to General Zhang, and she was alive and well. Lee Fang isn't dead!"

Off-the-books Operations Center

Outside Bethesda, Maryland

Leroux's jaw dropped at the revelation. The impossible revelation. He had heard the remains described. He had seen the photos. He had heard Morrison tell them that the DNA had been confirmed.

"Is that even possible?" he asked Tong who had been in the loop the entire two weeks he had been off. "Could we be wrong?"

Tong firmly shook her head. "Absolutely not. I read the report. They analyzed the remains and only found her DNA."

"Could they have, umm, chopped off a leg or something?" asked Tommy.

Again Tong shook her head. "No. They found different parts of her body. And he said alive and well. You're not alive and well if you're missing most of your parts." Her face firmed. "He has to be lying."

Kane stared at the camera in the room, clearly in turmoil at what he had just heard. "Chris, what-what's he saying? We're sure she's dead, right?"

Leroux's chest ached at the false hope on Kane's face. "Absolutely. He has to be lying. He's just buying time."

"Are you sure? One-hundred-percent sure?"

Leroux looked at Tong who gave a single firm nod of her head and responded. "Based on the report I read, the coroner was absolutely positive."

"That's good enough for me." Kane turned toward the bed, raising his weapon. "You're lying."

"No! No I'm not!"

"Then prove it."

"I-I can't. I mean, without you seeing her—"

"Where is she?"

"I-I don't know. We handed her over to General Zhang, then that's the last I saw of her. We reported back to our unit, were debriefed, then reassigned."

Leroux interrupted. "Dylan, ask him where the handoff happened. Was it in the open?"

"Where'd you hand her over?"

"Lanzhou."

"In a hangar? Outside?"

Wang's eyes bulged as he realized what Kane was asking. "Outside!"

"So she would have been visible?"

"Yes!" Wang's excitement was fleeting as he frowned. "But only if you had a satellite going by, and it was powerful enough to make her out."

"Where's Zhang based?"

"Urumqi."

"Is he always there?"

"He rarely leaves, but has been known to for Party business."

"Do you know anything about his security?"

Wang shook his head. "I've only been there the one time. I've never been assigned to the general before."

"Did you arrive by plane?"

"Yes."

"What type?"

"A Gulfstream, I think. Private jet."

"When?"

"The day after the kidnapping. Around eighteen-hundred-hours."

"And that's everything you know?"

"Yes! I swear!"

"I believe you." Kane put two in the man's head then turned to the camera. "Confirm his intel on the other five's locations. And find out where this General Zhang is."

Leroux watched Kane unscrew his suppressor. "What about Fang?"

"I don't believe him for a second, but check out what he said, just in case. Oh, and find out if there's any way to fake a DNA match."

Director Morrison's Office, CIA Headquarters

Langley, Virginia

Leroux sat across from Morrison in his office, not certain how to begin the hastily requested meeting. He had critical information obtained on an unauthorized op that had already resulted in two assassinations of Chinese operatives, one on Chinese soil.

He and the others could be in serious shit if Morrison didn't take well to the revelation.

"So, to what do I owe the honor? Shouldn't you be at the hospital?"

Leroux bit his lip. "I've, umm, shall we say, stumbled upon some information that I need help with."

Morrison leaned back in his chair, steepling his fingers, a slight smile on his face. "What have you guys found out?"

Leroux's heart skipped a beat. "What do you mean?"

"Kane is in Macao with Jack. You, Sonya, and Thomas Granger are holed up in one of Kane's secret bunkers, and you're all eliminating the Chinese team one by one."

Leroux snapped his jaw shut. "How-how do you...I mean, what would make you say that?"

"You don't become the National Clandestine Service Chief for the CIA without knowing a thing or two. Remember, I used to be operational."

Leroux frowned, his entire body weakening. "Don't punish Sonya. She was just helping out of loyalty to me. And Tommy didn't know—"

Morrison held up a hand, cutting him off. "Nobody is getting punished. You're doing what I would have done in your situation, though if I'm put in front of Congress, I won't admit that."

"I understand. We'll face the consequences on our own."

Morrison wagged a finger. "No, that's not what I meant. I mean I'll tell them you were all following my orders."

As much as Leroux was relieved to hear Morrison's words, he couldn't allow it. "I can't let you do that, sir. None of us would want to see you get in trouble for something you didn't know about."

Morrison regarded him for a moment. "Who do you think tipped off Kane? Who do you think sent Jack to help him?"

Leroux's eyes shot wide. "It was you?"

"Who else? How many knew we found Han Zhanshu?" Morrison leaned forward. "Now, what's going on?"

"There's a possibility that Lee Fang might still be alive."

It was Morrison's turn to be shocked. "What makes you think that?"

"When we interrogated Wang Keqiang, he made the claim, and provided us with some intel that might verify it. Unfortunately, we can't confirm it with the limitations of Dylan's setup."

"What do you need?"

"Satellite coverage of the Lanzhou Airbase in China from two weeks ago."

Morrison regarded him for a moment. "Do what you need to do, but I think all you're going to be doing is disproving a desperate man's delaying tactics." He eyed Leroux. "Did it work?"

"For a few minutes, then Dylan put two bullets in his skull."

Morrison chuckled. "Remind me to never get on his bad side. Did I tell you about the time he went rogue and broke into my house without my security team knowing?"

"I've heard the story."

"I feel for him. I hope for his sake he doesn't believe there's a possibility Fang is still alive."

Leroux sighed, shrugging. "He says he doesn't, but I think he might. I could see it in his eyes." He shifted in his chair. "What if it's true?"

"How can it be? We found the remains, the analysis was thorough. The DNA matched. It had to be her."

"Is there any way they could have faked it?"

Morrison shook his head then stopped. "I don't think so, but I'm not the expert." He leaned over and picked up his phone. "Have Dr. Castro-Diaz report to my office immediately."

JW Marriott Hotel

Hong Kong Special Administrative Region, China

Kane lay across the table repositioned beside the window, a small hole cut through the glass allowing his sniper rifle and scope a view of their target's hotel room across the street. Their target, Lin Biming, was staring out the window at the pro-democracy protests below, shaking his head.

"I get the impression he's not on their side," observed Jack from his perch behind the curtains, peering through a set of binoculars.

"Ya think?"

"Do you want to take bets on when the Chinese Tiananmen this place?"

"Not really. I'm afraid I'll win, and I'm not going to profit off something like that."

Jack grunted. "Yeah, I guess you're right. No bets, but do you think they will?"

Kane shifted his view slightly. "Definite possibility. The Chinese did it thirty years ago and look what happened. Nothing. The world condemned them, then signed trade deals and moved all their factories there. Western economies are too closely linked with China to do anything anymore. China could roll in here tomorrow and slaughter tens of thousands, the world will feign outrage, and after a suitable period of trade sanctions, their economies won't be able to take it, and consumers will be complaining that the price of their TVs have gone up too high. Two years tops, and things will be back to normal, and the Chinese will have proven they can get away with anything."

Jack sighed. "I'm afraid you might be right. If there's a country the BDS movement should be targeting, it's the Chinese. They're far worse than anything the Israeli's are accused of."

Kane growled. "Don't get me started on that."

Tong chirped in his ear. "Room 904. Putting you through now."

Kane adjusted his mike and watched as Lin answered the hotel phone by his bed. "Hello?"

Kane responded in perfect Chinese. "Hello, Mr. Lin. Two weeks ago you killed a friend of mine."

Lin grunted. "You'll have to narrow it down. I've killed a lot of people."

"Lee Fang."

Lin laughed. "That traitorous bitch? She deserves what's coming to her."

Kane paused at the choice of words, taking his finger off the trigger of his sniper rifle. "What do you mean?"

"I mean she deserved to die."

"You said 'what's coming to her.' Are you saying she's alive?"

"You're the one that said she's dead. Don't you know?"

Kane's entire body tensed as his pulse pounded. "Is she or isn't she dead?"

"The last I saw her, she was alive, but I'm sure she's dead by now. If she isn't, then you're too late to save her. She'll be dead the moment I hang up this phone."

Kane moved his finger back into place. "I don't think so." He squeezed, and Lin dropped to the floor, a spray of blood staining the white sheets behind him.

Director Morrison's Office, CIA Headquarters

Langley, Virginia

"I hate to admit this, but it's possible."

Both Leroux and Morrison reacted at the same time. "What?"

Morrison waved a hand in front of him. "Wait a minute. You're saying it's possible to fool a DNA match?"

Dr. Lucia Castro-Diaz shook her head. "No, that's not what I'm saying. What I'm saying is it's possible that our victim is still alive, and that we found the body of someone else with her DNA."

Leroux sank in his chair, shaking his head. "That makes no sense. You're saying what? That we found her twin?"

Castro-Diaz wagged her hand. "Not at all. What I'm saying is it is possible for two people, *not* twins, to have the same DNA."

Morrison shot up out of his chair. "What the hell are you talking about? Everything we've been told says that's impossible. Billions to one. Are you saying this is that billion to one shot?"

Castro-Diaz smiled. "No, not at all. What I'm saying is scientists have recently discovered something we hadn't realized. It's extremely rare, but it matches up with some odd intel we received a few years ago out of China."

"What was that?"

"They took bone marrow from thousands of key personnel. High-ranking military, government, important public figures." She paused. "And Special Forces personnel."

Leroux's eyebrows rose. "Like Lee Fang?"

Castro-Diaz turned to him. "Is she Chinese Special Forces?"

"She was at the time."

"Then there is a distinct possibility that she had her bone marrow taken, and from what you're telling me, I think it's a certainty."

"But what could bone marrow do? Are you saying that's what we found? A bunch of bone marrow peppered over someone else's remains?"

Castro-Diaz shook her head. "No, that's not at all what I'm saying. There is no doubt that those remains you found actually belong to someone who has her DNA. There's *no* doubt. This wasn't cross-contamination, deliberate or otherwise."

Morrison growled, returning to his seat. "Then just what the hell are you saying, Doctor?"

"We've recently discovered that in some people, when you give them a bone marrow transplant, the recipient's DNA can be completely overwritten by the donor's over time. In the end, they both have the same DNA."

"Are you kidding me?" Morrison leaned forward. "Are you telling me that if I get a bone marrow transplant from Chris, in a couple of years I'll have his DNA?"

"It's a possibility, yes."

"So, if I commit a crime, leave *his* DNA behind, the courts, which have come to rely upon the infallibility of DNA results, could accuse Chris of being the perpetrator instead of me?"

"In theory, yes. The odds are astronomical that someone who received a bone marrow transplant would then go out and commit a crime that relied upon DNA evidence for a conviction, but yes, it is theoretically possible."

Leroux exchanged a stunned glance with Morrison. This changed everything. It meant that every single body they had identified over the years through DNA, could be someone else.

But it would mean planning well in advance.

He turned to Castro-Diaz. "So, what you're saying is that the body we found, assuming Lee Fang is still alive, is someone who received her bone marrow."

"It's a definite possibility, especially since she was Chinese Special Forces. We believe they have a program in place where they take multiple 'volunteers,' usually prisoners, and give them the transplant, then when one takes, they use the recipient to replace the actual person, kill them in a manner such as what happened here, and no one is the wiser. This isn't a widely known thing, and people are hesitant to talk about it, because you'll have every homicidal maniac and pedophile out there trying to donate their bone marrow so they'll have reasonable doubt if ever caught.

We're trying to figure out a way to distinguish the two individuals, but at the moment, we don't have a way."

Leroux closed his eyes for a moment, processing the information. He stared at Castro-Diaz. "So, what you're saying is that Lee Fang could very well be alive."

"Yes."

Unknown Location

The sting of yet another smack woke Lee Fang from the few minutes of sleep she had managed to slip in before the camera monitoring her alerted the guards to her faux pas. The glaring lights, and a cacophony of sounds mixed together blaring from a loudspeaker in the corner, had kept her awake for most of her stay, but even that wasn't working anymore.

Though the back of a hand still did.

At first, the knowledge Kane and their friends would stop at nothing to retrieve her had sustained her, then had come the crushing revelation.

They thought she was dead.

She had never understood at the time why her bone marrow had been taken several years ago, but now she did. The moment she had betrayed her country, the protocol had been implemented with several female prisoners injected with her bone marrow, and apparently the process had worked on one, the woman's DNA rewritten to match Fang's. It was something she had never known was possible, but apparently, she was living proof the world thought her dead.

And she wasn't certain how she felt about that.

On the one hand, poor Kane would think her dead, so he could have closure, yet on the other, it meant no one was searching for her. There was no hope of rescue. And there was no hope of escape.

She was alone.

Fortunately, for the moment, she hadn't been physically tortured. It was all mental. She hadn't been allowed to sleep, her senses overwhelmed with harsh lights and sounds, and every hour on the hour she was interrogated, the questions always the same.

What had she told, and whom had she told it to?

And her answer was always the same.

The truth.

She had told everything she knew about the coup attempt and China's involvement, but nothing else. And she told it to her intake processor in the United States, someone she assumed was CIA, but couldn't be certain. Since then, she had been left alone by the US government. The matter had been buried, the Chinese involvement kept a secret, the military involvement as well, everything made to appear as if nothing had gone awry.

And the sheeple, for the most part, bought it.

Her life had gone on, as had those of the American public. Yet for some reason, General Zhang was rehashing the past, and in China, that meant something political was going on. Yet her brain was too fried to figure out what that might be.

All she knew was she was alone, and when they were finished with her, she'd be as dead as those she loved thought she was.

Off-the-books Operations Center

Outside Bethesda, Maryland

Tong busied herself making the travel arrangements for Kane's next target while Tommy compiled a list of all Gulfstream aircraft that had left the United States after the attack, and arrived in China within the next two days.

The list was long and growing.

Tong's phone rang and she swiped her thumb. "Go ahead."

"We're official again. It turns out there *is* a possibility she is alive. A doctor here says it involves bone marrow transplants."

Tong sat upright, stunned. "You're kidding me!"

"No, I'm as shocked as you are. I'm assembling the team. Get here as soon as you can."

She glanced at her partner. "And Tommy?"

"Send him home with our thanks. He'll get paid as per the last time."

"Understood. I'll be there within an hour. I have to do a proper shutdown here."

"Good. See you soon."

She ended the call and turned to Tommy. "Well, we're done here."

Tommy appeared a mix of disappointed and relieved. "Did they get her?"

"Not yet, but we're back on the books, so we're shutting this little operation down."

Tommy appeared subdued. "Okay, I understand. Umm, will you let me know what happens? I mean, if Fang is okay?"

Tong began shutting down the equipment in sequence. "If I can, I will."

"Thanks." Tommy initiated several shutdown procedures of his own, the entire system in standby mode within minutes. They left the storage container and Tong locked the door, scanning the area to make sure they were alone before heading for her car. They both climbed in and she handed him the hood.

"Really? You guys still don't trust me?"

She put the car in gear and pulled toward the road. "It's for your own protection. This way if anyone asks, you can honestly say you always wore a hood and never knew where you were taken."

He paled slightly. "Do you think that could happen?"

"This is the spy business. Anything can happen."

He quickly pulled the hood over his head. "I'm not sure I like this business anymore."

Operations Center 2, CIA Headquarters

Langley, Virginia

With the proper access, things were rapidly progressing, and Leroux was getting excited. They had a shot of the Lanzhou Airbase at the time in question, but it was from a low angle, the satellite just leaving the coverage area. They had a shot of the tarmac with a Gulfstream jet parked, and several people deplaning.

Including one that might be a woman.

Morrison entered, immediately taking in the footage shown on the massive display. "Explain."

"We've found a plane that matches Wang Keqiang's description, plus people getting off, one of whom might be a woman."

"And this is the best shot we have?"

"Unfortunately. Everything fits what Wang said, but we can't be certain. It's just too low an angle and too far. They probably knew exactly where our satellites were and timed it perfectly."

Morrison agreed. "Definitely a possibility."

"What do you want us to do?"

"This seems to check out, so we have to pursue it. If this bit was right, then it's likely General Zhang was there as well. If he went to this much trouble to get her, then I don't think he's going to let her get too far out of sight. Find out where he's been over the past two weeks. Most likely Fang is at one of those locations." Morrison headed for the door. "And find out what connection those two have. There has to be a *very* good reason why he's risking war over an exile that poses no threat to China anymore."

Urumqi Training Center

Urumqi, China

General Zhang sat back in his chair, his boots propped up on the corner of his desk as he watched the video feed from Lee Fang's latest interrogation, the results the same as the hundreds that had preceded this one.

It was growing tiresome, yet she was strong.

"I don't think she has anything left to tell," he said to his aide, standing at ease in front of his desk.

"I agree, General. I believe we can safely rule her out as a threat."

Zhang exhaled, staring at the woman he had gone to so much trouble to acquire. She was the only one who might threaten his future plans, though killing her wasn't enough. He had to know who she had told. Her escape from China had been swift and clearly organized by the Americans.

And it meant she likely had no time to tell anyone here.

But in America, their enemy had access to her for years.

And that could pose a problem.

Should he attempt to gain the power he sought, it would send the Americans into a panic. They wouldn't want a man like him in the presidency, as he would stand up to them on the world stage, and take China through the 21st century where in the end, it would be the dominant power on the planet, eclipsing the United States and its allies.

The future wasn't democracy, it was China's hybrid socialist-capitalist system.

Already, with the Belt and Road initiative, China was wielding its power in the poorest regions of the planet, spreading its technology and military influence to regions abandoned by the United States and the defunct Soviet Union. Their economy was thriving, they had the largest population in the world in which to wield their influence, with millions of loyal subjects spread across the world should a Fifth Column become necessary.

There was nothing like the threat of torturing loved ones back home to encourage a former citizen to do China's bidding.

China needed to stop worrying about the West. It was strong enough to take on any foes, and nonsense like Hong Kong couldn't be allowed to continue. He had proven how to deal with these problems. Swiftly. Strongly. He had taken care of Tibet, and was now dealing with the Muslim problem in the western part of his great nation.

Some were uncomfortable with his approach, though they dared not speak up. He was arguably the second most powerful man in the country, and no one would risk opposing him.

For if anyone were to replace the current leader, it would be him.

But only if no one knew he had been behind the coup attempt in the United States. Should that become common knowledge, the American public would become outraged, trade sanctions and other actions might be taken against his country, and the Party would move swiftly to deal with him for his unauthorized actions.

The few who had known were already dead or rotting in one of his detention centers, yet the Americans who might know were out of his reach for now. Which meant he had to know for certain Lee Fang hadn't told the Americans about him.

For he was certain his time was about to come. Hong Kong and Beijing's inaction on the matter was just the first mistake. There would be more. And with each challenge to Beijing's authority, more of the Party that supported a strong hand would look to him to provide it.

The beautiful thing about the Hong Kong situation was that it was no win. If troops were sent in to quell the riots, then Beijing would lose on the world stage, their economy would suffer initially, and he could use that to take over. If they didn't, he could play the President off as weak, and get the hardliners on his side, and still take over. This was his opportunity, an opportunity in planning for years.

When he had returned from Tibet and taken charge of the Muslim problem in the western part of the country, he had succeeded by showing no quarter. When he was finished, there wouldn't be a Muslim left. He'd destroy their religion, drum it out of their children, and within a generation or two, what he had started would end with the Muslim population eradicated, not through mass murder like the Nazis did, but by mass reeducation.

It would work.

It *was* working.

And who cared if he used the facilities at his command to hold a few of his own enemies. Like Lee Fang. When she had killed General Yee and fled to America with what she knew, he had begun to plan for her return. The prisoners were injected with her bone marrow—a project he had started—and when the DNA of one of their subjects had been successfully overwritten, that person was treated with kid gloves.

Until they were needed.

Like now. With the current crisis demanding he take action, Fang had been retrieved and the volunteer executed horribly, burned alive for the Americans to find. After all, they couldn't have some trace of poison or a bullet wound found. They had to find the burned remains of a woman with Lee Fang's DNA.

And it had worked brilliantly.

He had her in his own facility, steps away, and the Americans had buried a prisoner of such little importance, he didn't even know her name. Nor did he know the name of the man who now had his own DNA flowing through his system. His double had been created several years ago, just in case. If things went wrong for him, he wanted to leave the world thinking he was dead, while in reality, he'd be living the high-life—quietly—in the Caribbean or somewhere else more desirable than western China.

Everything had been thought of.

Every contingency prepared for.

He just needed to know what Fang had revealed of his involvement in the coup attempt, and who knew what. For he couldn't risk anyone using that information against him when he implemented his plan.

He turned to his aide. "If she doesn't reveal anything else by the end of day tomorrow, kill her, and make sure there's not a strand of her DNA left to find."

Beijing, China

Kane's Shaws of London cover had once again successfully delivered him through the front door of China. And now that he was back on the books, his concern about any challenges to his persona were gone.

I wonder if Jack made it.

They had traveled separately, as they had to Macao and Hong Kong, and were to rendezvous shortly.

Kane lowered the divider separating him from the limo driver sent by the hotel. "Pull over just ahead, please. I want to grab a bite to eat in the market."

The driver glanced at him in the rearview mirror. "Are you certain, sir? The hotel has excellent restaurants."

Kane smiled. "I have no doubt, but I'm craving some street food." He pointed ahead. "Here's fine." He handed him a couple of hundred yuan. "Take my luggage to the hotel. I'll be along in a little while."

"I can wait, sir."

Kane shook his head. "No, I want to stretch my legs after that flight. I'll grab a taxi later. Don't worry, I come to Beijing all the time. I know this city like the back of my hand." He stepped out and strolled through the busy market, then when the limo was out of sight, made his way to Li's Photo, miraculously still in business despite no one using film or digital cameras anymore.

Kane entered the CIA front and Chan Chao, its owner and his longtime contact, appeared startled to have a customer.

Chan frowned. "Oh, it's you."

"Don't act so happy to see me."

Chan grunted, rounding the counter and locking the front door, flipping a sign indicating they were closed. "Whenever you show up, it means work."

Kane took in his surroundings. "Maybe if you learned to repair smartphones, you'd have some business to keep you occupied."

Chan spat. "I'm old! I want to retire! But as long as you people keep coming here for my help, I'll never be allowed to."

Chan's wife Bing held aside the beads separating the store from the private area at the rear of the shop. She brightened at seeing Kane. "I no want him to work. If he busy, no time for jiggy-jiggy." She thrust her hips several times. "Then we both bored."

Kane laughed then stopped when someone knocked at the front door. Coded.

"That'll be Jack."

Chan left, returning a few moments later with the man with no surname.

"Any problems?"

Jack shook his head. "Nada. I think I've spent more time in China than I have the US over the past five years."

Kane sighed. "Yeah, me too."

"Enough chitchat," said Chan. "The sooner you two are out of here, the sooner I can go to bed. Do you want to see your equipment?"

"Yup. Secure comms?"

Chan pointed at a large black case sitting on a table and Kane snapped it open, smiling at the impressive care package from Langley. He fit an earpiece in place.

"Control, this is Arrow. Come in, over."

Chan's eyebrows rose at the unusual callsign. It had been Fang's when she was active, and he had chosen it for the revenge mission in her honor.

"Arrow, Control. We read you," replied Leroux.

"Tell me you've got something for me."

Operations Center 2, CIA Headquarters
Langley, Virginia

"Zhang is our primary target, so we're keeping a close tab on him as a matter of course," explained Leroux as he briefed Kane and Jack. "He's one of the most powerful generals in the country, and before his current assignment, was responsible for some pretty harsh crackdowns in Tibet. After his success there, he was assigned to western China to deal with the Uyghur problem."

"Oh, he's that guy, is he?"

"Yup. He's responsible for their 'Vocational Education and Training Centers.' Current estimates have anywhere from one million to three million people confined to these facilities, none with due process of course. There are at least a million Muslims, plus other religious minorities and various undesirables."

"Do we think Fang is in one of these facilities?"

"It's a possibility. If we assume it was Fang that we saw on that footage, then it's also reasonable to assume he went to wherever she was going to be held to oversee her interrogation."

"And?"

"And he left the airport via his own plane about thirty minutes later. We can't confirm she was on board because the plane was inside a hangar, and when it arrived at its destination, it taxied into another one. But here's the thing. In the past two weeks, he hasn't ventured more than ten miles from his destination."

"Which was?"

"The Urumqi Training Center."

"And it's one of these camps?"

"It is. It's directly under his command, and no one questions his methods because the leadership feels it's working."

Kane sighed. "Yet the world sits by and says nothing."

"Hey, the public wants their cheap electronics, not human rights for people in a country they'll never see."

"What a lovely world we live in. Okay, so if we assume she's there, is there any way to get her out, or even just confirm she's there?"

Leroux stared at the displays at the front of the operations center. "We have satellite imagery of the facility that I've sent you via a secure message. We know almost nothing about what's inside beyond a few witness reports. It's well guarded, though they rely heavily on fear and electronic measures. You're not facing hundreds of soldiers. From what we can tell, perhaps fifty guards with hundreds of staff who probably don't pose a problem beyond raising the alarm."

"Okay, keep prying. I'm going to need to see this place for myself."

"I'll arrange it, however you can't go as you."

"I know. It's time to use the Face/Off machine."

Leroux chuckled. "Are you Travolta or Nick Cage?"

Jack's voice cut in. "He sounds more like Statham from Spy."

Child snorted. "Love that movie."

Leroux agreed. "Chan is fully equipped. He'll set you up. Good luck."

Urumqi Training Center

Urumqi, China

Fang sat on the edge of her bed, her head drooping. She had learned if she lay down, she'd fall asleep instantly, and the guards would be there moments later to wake her. But if she fell asleep sitting up, it would often take them several minutes to figure it out, and those few minutes, added together, might help get her through this.

Though to what end, she wasn't sure.

She would eventually be executed. The only question was when.

The door opened and a general entered, and on instinct she stood at attention before remembering where she was. She returned to her bed and her stupor.

"Do you know who I am?"

She shook her head.

"My name is General Zhang Quanguo. Have you heard of me?"

The name sounded familiar, and she struggled to remember where she had heard it before, her mind mud. Then it clicked. "The men who kidnapped me said it. They said you thanked me for my service." She squinted at him. "But I never served under you."

"They weren't talking to you. They were talking to the woman who died in your place."

She tried to shake some sense into her brain. "I-I don't understand."

"And you don't need to. You won't be alive long enough to care."

Fang smiled.

Relief at last.

"I can end your suffering. All you need to do is tell me what I want to know."

"I've already told you everything I know."

"Have you?"

She stared up at him. "What's changed? You've always known where I was, right? Why take me now?" Her mind finally filled in the blanks of who this man actually was, his well-known record replaying in her head. Her jaw dropped. "You're planning to make a move, aren't you?"

He chuckled. "Clever girl."

"What are you planning?"

"Nothing that concerns you."

"If it affects my country, it does."

"This isn't your country anymore. You betrayed it, and allied yourself with the Americans."

"I'll always be Chinese. And I didn't betray my country. You and I both know what happened wasn't sanctioned by the Party. It was

General Yee who was behind this." She stared at him, her eyes widening. "And you! You were involved, weren't you?"

Zhang smiled. "Again, clever girl. Did you tell anyone that?"

She shook her head. "I didn't know until now."

"So then no one knows I was the one behind it."

"No."

"Good." He put a hand on the doorknob. "Your execution is scheduled for midnight tomorrow. I see no need to move it up. It will give you some time to contemplate what you have done, and how much you, a traitor to your country, the Party, and your unit, deserve to die a most horrible death."

Li's Photo

Beijing, China

Kane stared in the mirror at himself, shaking his head. "This tech is amazing. Every time I use it, I have to remind myself it's really me under there."

Jack agreed. "The worst is when you catch a glimpse of yourself in a mirror or a reflection in a window. The first few times, I nearly shit myself and blew my cover."

"Yeah, I know the feeling." Kane turned to face the Chans. "How do I look?"

Bing gave him the twice over. "Good enough to eat. Come to bed with me, I show you."

Kane laughed. "As tempting as that sounds, I've got a train to catch. Jack? You can catch a later one if you want."

Bing grinned and Jack appeared at a loss for words. "Umm, ahh." He threw up his hands. "What the hell do I say that won't hurt her feelings?"

"You say, sure!" cried Bing. "Old woman experienced. Know lots of tricks." Her eyebrows bobbed suggestively. "One night with me, you never go back to those young girls. You be a changed man."

Kane remained silent, loving the exchange that for once wasn't aimed at him.

Chan shook his head. "Woman, one of these days someone is going to take you up on your offer, then what are you going to do?"

She snapped at him. "Enjoy myself for a change."

Chan handed Kane a clean phone. "Your tickets are on here, along with your hotel confirmation, and a fake email registering your new phone, acknowledging your old one on your account had been lost. That way you have an explanation for having no photos or any history on it. Study your covers, and keep to yourselves. Those clothes you have on suggest you're laborers. You're going back to visit family for a week. All your equipment is standard issue." Chan jabbed a finger at both of them. "Be careful. Where you're going is covered with cameras. Always assume you're being watched, even on the shitter. Hell, even *in* the shitter."

"Got it. This isn't my first rodeo."

"What the hell do horses have to do with anything?"

Kane laughed. "We've got to get you a dictionary of American slang, buddy."

Chan batted away the suggestion with his hand. "Bah, I hate to read. Too many words. Now get out of here before my wife starts taking her clothes off. I don't want you two starting something I have to finish."

Operations Center 2, CIA Headquarters

Langley, Virginia

"Anything?"

Child shook his head at Leroux. "It's not like they've got American equipment there that we've built a back door into."

Leroux sighed. "There are advantages to being a totalitarian state in our business."

"Are you saying we're on the wrong side?"

"Nooo, I'm saying they're not playing fair, and we're stupid."

Child's head bobbed. "I could go along with that." He motioned at his station. "I've got access to lots of camera feeds that aren't official, but they won't show us anything. We have nothing inside the prison, and I don't see how we're going to get anything."

Leroux chewed his cheek. "That means Kane is going in blind."

Child stared at him. "He's going in?"

Tong gave Child a look. "How do you think he's going to rescue her? Knock on the front gate and ask them to send her out?"

"Hadn't thought about that." Child folded his arms. "Unfortunately, until he gets on location, I don't think there's much we can do. When he gets there, he can deploy a microdrone or two, and maybe we'll get lucky. If he could tap into one of the comms lines, then we could get really lucky. Until then, we're up shit's creek."

Unfortunately, Leroux had to agree.

En route to Urumqi, China

Kane sat in his seat on the highspeed train, saying nothing. He curled toward the window, pulling his hat down low, prepping for feigned sleep. He was tired enough for it to perhaps turn into the real thing if he wasn't careful.

He was an emotional wreck. The possibility that Fang might be alive had him excited and relieved, but also terrified of the possibility that it might all be a lie. All they had was a poor shot of what might be a woman getting off a plane at the right place and time. In all honesty, if it weren't for the fact that person might be the love of his life—the lost love—he would give it little credence.

Then there was the possibility it was true, and how long it had been. More than two weeks had passed. If it had indeed been her, how long would her captor keep her alive? The intent obviously hadn't been to kill her outright, which meant they wanted to question her, or make an example of her. Either way, would they wait two weeks before they finally executed her? And with what he and Jack had just done over the past few days, would they risk waiting any longer?

His very actions might have sealed her fate.

They had eliminated three of those responsible, leaving only four from the strike team. If he successfully rescued her alive—*if*—he'd let the others live. They had just been doing their jobs, and wouldn't have killed anybody if this new intel was correct.

This willingness to forgive had him questioning his previous actions. It was the exact reason he wasn't supposed to go rogue, to take revenge on his own. Mistakes could be made. The three men he had killed were bad, perhaps innocent of killing Fang, though definitely guilty of beating Sherrie nearly to death—an action he strongly believed deserved death. He had no real regrets about killing them, though hoped no one on his side would pay the price down the road when the roles were reversed.

It was their boss, General Zhang, that had to die no matter what. He could never be allowed to try this again. But he had to keep that desire to himself. If Langley knew he planned to kill one of the most powerful men in China, they'd go apeshit.

He spotted Jack taking his seat a few rows ahead, feigning sleep as well. The ride was eighteen hours. If they could manage to avoid any contact, they should be free and clear. A young man sat beside him and Kane acknowledged him with a nod.

Then took a chance.

He pulled out his phone, unlocked it, then disabled the sleep mode. Bringing up the ticket, he turned to the man. "I need to sleep desperately.

It's been a hard month's work, and I want to be fresh when I see my family. Can you show them my ticket for me when they come by?"

The young man shrugged. "Sure."

"Thanks." Kane put the phone on his tray table then resumed his sleep pose, soon drifting off, images of an imagined reunion with Fang leaving a smile on his face.

Urumqi Training Center
Urumqi, China

Fang stirred as the door to her cell opened, a tray of food brought in along with some water. She glanced at the clock on the wall and was shocked to see she had been asleep for over twelve hours. After Zhang had left the room, the lights had been turned off, just a soft one over the door now casting a gentle glow, and the loudspeaker had remained off. No one had come in to slap her awake, and she had unknowingly taken advantage of it.

I guess this is how you're treated when they find out you knew nothing all along, and have only hours left to live.

She said nothing, waiting for the guard to leave, then attacked the food, at least partially satisfying a ravenous hunger. Her stomach full, she lay back in her bed, picturing the love of her life on her closed eyelids, hearing his laughter, feeling his lips pressed against hers, relishing in the love they had shared for too brief a time. She had sacrificed everything to right an injustice, and she had no regrets, at least not when it came to that.

She just wished she had been given one last chance to say goodbye.

Urumqi Beijiao Passenger Transport Terminal
Urumqi, China

Kane awoke to someone shaking him, and was about to strike out when he caught himself, realizing it was his seatmate.

"Isn't this your stop?"

Kane peered out the window then quickly stood. "Yes, thanks." He chastised himself for sleeping for so long, though it was clear he needed the rest, and over the next few hours, he would need to have not only his wits about him, but a body ready for anything.

He stepped onto the platform and spotted Jack nearby. They retrieved their luggage, merely meager possessions designed to fit their cover, then headed to their hotel in separate taxis, checking into separate rooms. He performed a quick scan for any bugs, finding none active.

Chan's people are good.

A coded knock at the door indicated Jack's arrival. He opened it and for a moment his heart raced, the face of a Chinese laborer smiling at him. He let him in then locked the door behind him.

"These masks are a little too good sometimes."

Jack motioned at the room in general. "Are we good?"

"Yup. Everything has been cleaned or bypassed. It's safe to talk."

Jack dropped into a chair. "Mine's clear too. Your friend Chan has some competent people."

"He's been in the business for forty years. He knows everything and everyone. He's one of our most reliable conduits in and out of the country. Not just for equipment, but people as well."

"I'm impressed so far."

Kane reached under the bed and pulled out two large cases. "His people are supposed to have left us some toys that security on the train might not have found appropriate for two laborers to have."

Jack's eyes brightened. "Ooh! I've been to Vegas! Are we talking something naughty?"

"You had your chance with Wang and you blew it."

"That's not how I remember it."

Kane snorted as he opened one of the cases, Jack rising and unlocking the other.

Both whistled.

Jack picked up a Glock. "You gotta love Chan."

"You've never worked with him before?"

Jack shook his head. "No, I've got my own guy in Beijing." He started rummaging through the supplies. "I might have to switch guys."

Kane paused his own inventorying, glancing at Jack. "Just remember, when you work with Chan, you work with his wife."

Jack stared at him. "She *is* just joking, right? I mean, she was relentless."

Kane chuckled. "I think she's voracious, but faithful, though you never know. That 'no last name' thing you've got going might just rev up her engine a little too high."

Jack frowned. "I think I'm going to stick with my guy."

"Good idea." Kane grinned as he held up a tiny device. "Microdrones! I love these things. You need to be within range to use them, but almost nobody notices them. These will come in handy." He stepped over to the window and peered out. "You know, I think we might be in range to at least get some outside surveillance footage. The signal would drop off too much if we tried to go inside a building, but it might give us an idea where she's being held."

Jack grabbed the controller. "Dibbs."

Operations Center 2, CIA Headquarters
Langley, Virginia

"Control, do you copy?"

Leroux breathed a sigh of relief at the long-awaited check-in. It had been almost nineteen hours since he had last heard from Kane, and until this moment, they had no idea if he was still on mission, or arrested for spying back in Beijing. He adjusted his headset. "Five-by-five, Arrow. I assume this means you're in position?"

"Confirmed. Our friend provided a burst-mode satellite uplink. We should be able to communicate without anyone figuring out where we are. We've just deployed microdrones. We're going to be uploading the data to you, but at a reduced frame rate. There's no way this equipment is going to be able to send you full motion. If you see something interesting, let us know, and we'll send you more complete data."

Leroux turned to Child who pointed to the displays at the front of the room, half a dozen feeds appearing, showing about a frame per second. "Confirmed, we're receiving your feeds now."

235

"Good. Any word on Sherrie?"

Leroux tensed. "No change."

"Sorry to hear that. Well, let's get Fang back home and maybe hearing her voice will bring her out of it. If I know her, she's beating herself up inside over thinking she failed."

Leroux's eyes burned. "Sounds…like a plan. Be careful with how much data you're sending us. Too many data bursts and you're traceable."

"You're right." The displays went dark. "If we find anything, we'll send it to you."

"Good thinking."

"Arrow, out."

Leroux dropped in his seat and Tong left her station, taking a knee beside him, her voice low.

"Are you okay?"

He nodded, though it was a lie.

"Why don't you go to the hospital? Spend some time with her. If anything happens here, I'll patch you in, and you can be here inside of fifteen minutes."

He shook his head. "No, my place is here."

"You've got a good team. Let us help you."

He stared at her for a moment then drew a quick, deep breath, holding it for several seconds. He exhaled. "You're right. I do." He rose and turned to the team. "I'll be gone for a bit, though I'll be on comms. Sonya's in charge while I'm gone."

"Say hi for us!"

"Give her a hug for me."

Leroux headed for the exit, saying nothing, tears threatening to escape as the well-wishes for the woman he loved, and the operative they all knew from missions together over the years, continued to be shouted by a team that had once intimidated him, but he now considered family.

Dushanzi Hotel
Urumqi, China

Jack gave the coded knock and Kane opened the door. "Any luck?"

Jack shook his head. "Nada. There are too many security cameras around the facility and too many personnel. They're trying to sell to the world that these are just places for the poor to get an education, so they're paranoid about anyone being able to prove different. I scanned the area and there were indications of sensors on all the manhole covers, everything. There's no way I can tap any communications lines. They've probably pressurized the lines as well. Cut into them, and they'll know."

Kane had to agree. "You're probably right."

"If I had more time, I could find a way, but the fact we've bumped off three of those involved already, something tells me they know we're coming."

Kane frowned. "Yeah, I was thinking that too. It probably wasn't a good idea in retrospect."

Jack shrugged. "Hey, we all thought she was dead. And now that we know she might not be, we've got a shot at getting her out. But if we're going to, we better be doing it now. If they haven't put two and two together yet, they soon will, and they'll probably finish the job sooner rather than later."

Kane pointed at the display. "Control just sent us this. That's General Zhang. He's left what Langley thinks is the main headquarters for the facility, and is heading into one of the barracks."

Jack peered at the overhead satellite shot on the tablet. "That one looks like it's nowhere near any of the other barracks that we know house the prisoners."

"Fifty bucks says this is where they keep their special guests. If it's true, that could be good for us."

Jack eyed him. "Why?"

"It's only a couple of hundred feet from the main gate, and that gate's the only way in that I can see."

Jack pointed at the image. "Yeah, but look at that place. Barbed wire, lights, guard towers, the works. The gate isn't exactly left open."

"No, but look in those suitcases. Those aren't Napoleonic army uniforms in there. We can bluff our way inside, get Fang, get out. Bibbidi-Bobbidi-Boo and we're done."

Jack rolled his eyes. "Riiight. With hundreds of Chinese troops on our asses."

"Hey, I didn't say the plan was perfect."

"You didn't say it was a plan, either."

Urumqi Training Center

Urumqi, China

Fang, startled awake by something, quickly rolled to a seated position on her bed, a thin mattress brought in earlier providing some welcome comfort in her final hours. It wasn't the pillowtop with cooling gel she had back home with Kane, but it wasn't a concrete slab either.

Zhang entered and she rose, glancing at the clock.

Three hours left.

"I thought you should know I've moved up your execution."

She tensed. "Why?"

"Three of the men involved in your rendition have been killed. We believe your new masters at the CIA are behind it."

"And you're afraid one of your men talked?"

"My men are loyal to their country and the Party. They would never talk."

"Then why are you moving up the clock?"

"Merely a precaution. Besides, I have to go to Beijing for a morning meeting, and I want to witness the end of the great Lee Fang."

Her stomach was in knots, yet she kept her face devoid of emotion. "How much time do I have left?"

"My plane leaves in two hours. Make peace with whatever gods you might believe in. I'll be back after the arrangements have been made."

She hesitated a moment. "Umm, can I write a letter to someone?"

Zhang stared at her for a moment. "You're forgetting something."

"What?"

"You're already dead. Back in your new home. It will never get delivered, otherwise they'll know we tricked them."

"You could always say you let me write it before you killed me there."

He paused, apparently considering her request. "No. You didn't give General Yee any time to write a letter to his family. I see no reason why you should be afforded the opportunity you denied him."

He left the room, and a tear rolled down her cheek unnoticed as she returned to her bed and curled into a ball. She didn't feel sorry for herself. Not in the slightest. As the general said, she was dead already. She was always going to die, whether that was two hours from now or two years from now, and without Kane and her friends, none of it mattered.

She was alone, and would remain so.

In fact, two hours was a mercy. It would soon be over, and rather than wallow in self-pity, she instead thought of her training.

How to die as quickly as possible in a fire.

Breathe deeply, sear the lungs with the heat, and you'll suffocate to death within minutes.

Though those minutes would no doubt be the most agonizing of her life.

She rolled over, staring about the room for anything that might deny the general the satisfaction he sought.

Operations Center 2, CIA Headquarters

Langley, Virginia

"Uh oh."

Tong spun her chair toward Child. "What?"

"Well, you know how Zhang hasn't traveled more than ten miles from his current location for the past two weeks?"

Tong's body tensed for what she was certain was about to be bad news. "Yes?"

"Well, it looks like his plane is scheduled to leave in two hours for Beijing."

She drew a slow breath. "Any chance it's for someone else?"

"I don't think so." He tapped some keys then pointed at the displays, a limousine shown.

"What am I looking at?"

"This is the VIP transport for the airport. It left there a few minutes ago."

"Can we tell where it's headed?"

"Not yet, though it is heading in the right direction to pick up the general."

Tong shook her head. "Well, if Fang's alive, I have a funny feeling it won't be for long." She activated her comms. "Arrow, Control, come in, over."

Dushanzi Hotel

Urumqi, China

Kane stared at one of the microdrone's feeds with a good angle on General Zhang as he left the barracks, a smile on the man's face.

"That has to be where they're keeping her."

Jack glanced at him. "Are you willing to bet everything on that? Once we go in, we're committed. We won't get a second chance."

Kane's earpiece squawked. "Arrow, Control, come in, over."

"Go ahead, Control."

"Arrow, a flight plan for Zhang's private plane has just been filed. He's heading for Beijing in less than two hours."

Kane cursed. "Copy that. We believe Fang is being held in building A-3 on the map. What can you tell us about it?"

"Stand by."

Kane relayed what Jack had missed as he fit his own earpiece into place. "If he's leaving in two hours, and they know about the three operatives we eliminated, then he's killing her before he leaves, or he's taking her with him. Either way, we have to act now."

"Yeah, and we don't have two hours. You always have to be at your departure gate ninety minutes before your flight is scheduled to depart."

Kane rolled his eyes. "Let's assume we have tops one hour. We have to go now."

"You still haven't told me your plan."

Kane shrugged. "Wing it?"

It was Jack's turn to roll his eyes. "Yeah, like that's never backfired before."

Sonya finally responded. "Beyond dimensions, we can't tell you anything, sorry. We just have nothing on these facilities."

Kane frowned. "That's what I thought you were going to say. Arrow, out."

Inova Fairfax Hospital
Falls Church, Virginia

Leroux entered the hospital room, his stress level pegging the moment he saw Sherrie, still unconscious, still swollen, still covered in bandages. Yes, there had been progress over the past two weeks, and yes, when she finally woke she wouldn't have to endure the pain she might have if she had never gone into the coma, yet the selfish side of him would gladly trade all of that potential relief for her eyes to be open right now, rather than shut.

His comms squawked, and he held up a finger, cutting off his father about to greet him from his chair. "Go ahead."

"Sir, Kane and Jack are going in. Zhang is leaving for Beijing in less than two hours. You might want to get back here."

Leroux cursed. "Copy that, I'll be there in twenty minutes." He shook his head at his father. "Sorry, Dad, I've got to go. No time to explain."

"My son, the spy."

247

Leroux gave him a look. "Not quite." He quickly kissed Sherrie's forehead and whispered in her ear. "We think Fang is still alive. Dylan is going in to rescue her now. We should know shortly. I love you."

He headed out the door, breaking into a jog. Fang might be alive, but Kane could end up dead saving her unless he had the best team possible backing him up.

And that means my team with me running it.

He cursed his self-indulgence, and swore to never leave his post again.

Outside the Urumqi Training Center

Urumqi, China

Kane strode swiftly and with purpose toward the front gate, his colonel's uniform as prim and proper as any in the Chinese People's Liberation Army. Jack was dutifully to his left and two paces behind, just where an aide should be. The sun had set an hour ago, and the streets were fairly quiet, the facility apparently not a place the locals wanted to risk being around lest they find themselves on the wrong side of its walls.

Two spotlights focused on them and a challenge was issued. "Halt! Identify yourselves!"

Jack stepped forward, and responded in perfect Chinese. "I am Lt. Kuang, and this is my commanding officer, Colonel Liu. We are here to see General Zhang on urgent business from Beijing."

"Step forward with your identification."

They complied, their Chan-supplied papers produced to one of the guards as Type 95 assault rifles were focused on them. The papers were handed back and a smart salute executed.

Kane returned it.

"Do you have an appointment, Colonel?"

Kane shook his head. "No. Beijing felt it was too important to risk interception. Is the general here?"

"He is. I will call—"

Kane wagged a finger. "No. No calls. And don't record our arrival. This meeting will have never happened, and we were never here. Understood?"

The soldier's eyes bulged. "Yes, sir." He led them to a side entrance and they stepped through the thick walls. "I will escort—"

Kane held up a hand. "If you leave your post, then a record must be made. Man your post, Corporal. I'm quite familiar with where the general's office is."

The man bowed. "Yes, of course, Colonel." He snapped another salute and Kane returned it before walking briskly toward the main administration building. A slight bend in the road, and they were soon out of sight of the main gate. Kane headed for the side of one of the buildings and pulled out a cigarette while Jack retrieved his phone.

"Do you have control?"

"Yeah, all of them."

Kane smiled, the microdrones key to their success. "Have one monitor the front gate from overhead, one the main entrance to the admin building, and one the barracks."

Jack repositioned the drones. "Everything looks good for now."

"Okay, see if we can get in the barracks."

Jack sent a drone toward the building then shook his head. "The door's closed. I might be able to get in through the ventilation system, but I don't think we've got that kind of time."

"Agreed." Kane stamped out his cigarette, the ruse over, the vile taste one he hated every time he had to smoke as part of his cover.

Now, a good cigar…

They strode toward the barracks, unchallenged. Jack pulled on the door, and to both their surprise, it opened. Kane stepped in to find two guards about to challenge them when they noticed his rank.

"Is the general here?"

Both snapped to attention, one of them replying. "No, Colonel. He just left. I believe he returned to his office."

"And the prisoner?"

"We're prepping the room now. We'll be ready for her incineration before the general leaves."

Kane's stomach flipped at the possible implications of those words, yet he maintained control. "Excellent work. Which cell is she in? We have some final questions for her."

"Third door on the left, Colonel. The code is 4-2-4-1."

"Very good."

Kane and Jack strode down the hall and Kane entered the code, his heart hammering as the lock clicked. He still wasn't convinced Fang was alive. For all he knew, they were about to discover a completely different prisoner with only minutes to live on the other side of the door.

Yet the possibility had him nearly passing out from anticipation.

He pushed open the door, gasping in horror at the sight before him.

Fang lifted her sagging head as the door opened yet again, two officers she hadn't seen yet entering, one of them rushing toward her, his eyes wide with shock.

He's probably terrified of what Zhang will do to him if he's denied his execution.

Her wrists were cut, the blood flowing, a sharp edge under the table having done the trick.

"Fang! Oh my God, what have you done!" cried the colonel.

And she froze, her heart leaping at the voice. "Dylan?"

He grabbed her and hugged her, then pushed her back, pulling out a knife and slicing a strip off her bedsheet, quickly wrapping it around her left wrist.

"What are you doing here?"

The strange face glanced up at her as he bandaged her bleeding wrists. "Saving your ass, of course."

She assessed the other man, holding the door open an inch, watching for anyone approaching. "And him?"

The man gave her a two-fingered salute. "I'm Jack. Just Jack." He shrugged. "It's a long story."

Kane examined his handiwork then the blood on the bed. "You just did this, didn't you?"

"I, well, normally I wouldn't, but they were going to burn me alive in a few minutes, so I figured I wouldn't give them the satisfaction."

The strange face, so Chinese, smiled. "That's my girl."

She reached up and touched the mask. "I just can't believe it's you." She stood and straightened herself. "So, what's your plan for getting out of here?"

"We're winging it," replied Jack from the door, his tone suggesting he wasn't too pleased with the fact.

Kane shrugged. "Something always presents itself."

Jack stared at his phone, shaking his head. "You're one lucky bastard." He handed the phone to Kane. "Check the front gate. You were right."

Kane smiled then showed the phone to Fang, an overhead shot of a gate visible. "What am I looking at?"

"Microdrone footage of the front gate. That's General Zhang's car arriving to take him to the airport." He grinned. "And it's our ticket out of here."

Her eyes bulged. "Are you nuts?"

He extended his hand. "Hi, Dylan Kane. Have we met?"

She giggled then swooned, suddenly lightheaded. He grabbed her.

"Are you going to be okay?"

"I think so. But I need some food and water to help replace the blood I lost."

"As soon as we get out of here, we'll find a Circle K and grab some road snacks."

She gave him a big hug. "I thought I'd never see you again."

"Me neither." He leaned down and kissed her, and Jack cleared his throat.

"I'd say get a room, but I'd actually like to watch. How about we get out of here first, then we'll discuss terms."

Fang blushed, pulling away. "Maybe he's right." She leaned over so she could see him. "About the escaping thing, not the watching thing."

Jack frowned. "You're no fun."

Operations Center 2, CIA Headquarters

Langley, Virginia

Leroux burst into the operations center, out of breath from sprinting all the way from the parking garage. "Status?"

Tong rose from her station. "They've made entry. We have their drone footage, and the Chief approved a satellite retasking, so we now have coverage of the area for the next thirty minutes."

Leroux took his customary position at the center of the room, his eyes not for a moment leaving the display wrapping the front of the operations center as he took in as much as he could while Tong brought him up to date.

"The general's plane is leaving in less than two hours, and it looks like his limo just arrived to take him to the airport."

"And our people?"

"Inside the barracks." She tapped her keyboard and an indicator flashed, outlining the building. "They've been inside for about five minutes."

"Any sign they've been discovered?"

"No. They're disguised as a Chinese colonel and lieutenant, with full face masks and skin coloring. They entered the front gate no problem, claiming a covert mission to meet with the general."

"And they bought that?"

"Nothing like the fear of death or worse to stop someone lower on the chain from challenging a story."

Child spun in his chair, adding his two cents. "They probably don't get a lot of people trying to break *in*. Those defenses aren't designed to keep people out." He dropped his foot, killing his spin, puzzled. "So, just how do they expect to get out?"

Leroux jabbed a finger at the limo idling by the admin building. "If I know Kane, he's planning on taking her out through the front door."

Urumqi Training Center

Urumqi, China

Jack stepped into the hallway and beckoned the two guards at the door. "Come here." The two men exchanged confused glances. "Now! That's an order from the colonel!"

They both bounced several inches then bolted down the hallway. Jack held the door open then closed it behind them. Kane put the first in a sleeper hold, Jack doing the same with the other before either could react.

Within moments, both were out cold.

Kane pointed at the shorter one. "Strip him."

Jack looked askance at him. "You keep trying to get my rocks off with men. Do we need to discuss something?"

"It's for her, you tool. We can't just walk her out of here in her prison outfit, covered in blood."

Jack frowned as he dropped to his knees, beginning his assigned task. "If this dude is going commando, I'm going to be really upset."

Fang waved a hand. "Don't worry, I can go without. I go commando all the time."

Jack's eyebrows shot up then he glanced at Kane. "I see why you two are together."

They both gave him toothy smiles.

As each piece of clothing was removed, Fang put them on, and within minutes, she was fully outfitted.

And looked ridiculous.

She held out her arms, the sleeves sagging over her hands as she stared down at her legs. "Not exactly tailored for a woman my size."

"It'll have to do." Kane dropped to his knees, rolling up her pant legs as best he could as she went to work on the sleeves. "Remember. If we walk as if we belong here, no one will notice. It's night, there are not many people around"—Jack checked his phone and gave a thumbs up— "and we only have about a hundred feet to go. I'll open the rear door of the limo, you climb in, then me, then Jack. We put a gun on the driver, and Bob's your uncle, we're good. Ready?"

She nodded. "No. But let's go anyway."

One of the guards groaned and Jack kicked him in the head. "We better tie these two up first."

"So, you're into the kinky stuff. You and Wang really would have hit it off." Kane grabbed the sheet from the mattress and tossed it to him.

"Haw-haw. I guess we'll never know. You remodeled his skull, remember?"

Operations Center 2, CIA Headquarters
Langley, Virginia

"Is everything set?"

Chan's response sounded incredulous. "You mean it worked?"

Leroux smiled slightly. "Not yet, but if it's going to, it could be any minute now. Are your people ready?"

"Yeah, the underground railroad is ready, but it's not what you think."

Leroux tensed. "What do you mean?"

"Kane told me to send them east, not south."

Leroux's eyes shot wide. "East!" The entire room exchanged shocked looks. "Why the hell would he want to go into the most populous area?"

"Because he's loopy? Ask him when you see him."

Leroux cursed. "*If* I see him. Will you be able to monitor him?"

"No. Once he's in, I won't know anything until he comes out."

Leroux tensed. "And how long will that take?"

"About twenty-four-hours."

"And just where is he coming out?"

"You don't want to know."

Urumqi Training Center

Urumqi, China

Jack led the way down the hallway, sprinting toward the outer door with Kane and Fang on his heels. Jack had activated a signal jammer a moment before they entered the hallway in case anyone was monitoring the cameras, but anything more than a few seconds could raise suspicions.

As they reached the outer door, the phone on the wall rang. Jack eyed it. "Should we answer it?"

Kane shook his head, pushing open the door and stepping into the crisp night air. "No. There's probably a code."

"Won't they be looking for us then?"

"Maybe, but they'll never think to look inside the general's limo."

"I still think this plan is whack."

"Yup. Which is exactly why it's going to work. Do the unexpected, and they just might not be expecting it."

Jack gave him a look as they marched toward the limo. "Do you hear yourself sometimes?"

"No. I usually work alone. You're getting gold here." Kane strode directly toward the idling limo, blocking the driver's view of the loosely attired Fang, with Jack taking up the rear. Kane pulled on the door handle and cursed. It was locked. He tapped on the passenger side window. "Open the door."

The driver leaned over as the window lowered. "This car is for General Zhang."

Kane glared at him, tapping his rank insignia. "You don't think I'm fully aware of that? We're accompanying the general to the airport. Now unlock the door!"

"Yes, sir!" The lock clicked and Kane opened the door. Fang climbed inside then he followed, his "aide" joining them and closing the door. The passenger side window slowly rolled up.

Kane leaned forward. "Disable your speaker. We're about to have a classified conversation. If I find out you were listening in, I'll be sending your testicles to Beijing, and your body back to your family."

The driver's eyes bulged with fear and a trembling hand reached overhead, flicking several switches. "Yes, sir."

Kane pressed the switch to put the partition up. "Can you hear us?" There was no response, though an intelligent spy wouldn't have replied. Kane relaxed, leaning back in his seat, then pointed toward a small fridge. "Check and see what we've got for party supplies." He kept speaking Chinese, just in case. Jack leaned forward and opened the fridge then grinned. He handed out three Cokes, Fang eagerly snapping hers open then gulping it down, the sugary drink providing her with much-needed energy. Another cabinet was opened, and all manners of American junk food were revealed.

"Let's eat, shall we?" said Jack as he dove in. "Who knows when we'll get another chance?"

Operations Center 2, CIA Headquarters
Langley, Virginia

"I can't believe that worked!" exclaimed Child, his mouth agape, his head shaking as they all stared at the screen, their three targets, for the moment, safely ensconced in General Zhang's limo.

"Actually, I'm not too surprised," replied Leroux. "It's training and balls. They had the right disguises, they had confidence, and the element of surprise."

"I hate to rain on the parade," said Tong, "but it looks like we've got some activity."

Leroux frowned, rising from his station. "What?"

Tong pointed at two guards running toward the barracks and Leroux cursed.

"Okay, patch me in."

Tong tapped some keys then gave a thumbs up.

"Arrow, Control. The shit might be about to hit the fan. You've got two hostiles running to the barracks you just left, over."

"Understood," replied Kane. "Just let me know if you see the general or anyone else coming toward the car."

"Copy that. How's Fang?"

"She's alive, so let's keep her that way."

Leroux smiled at the joy in Kane's voice.

From your lips to God's ears.

Urumqi Training Center
Urumqi, China

An alarm sounded and Kane lowered the divider, reaching forward and pushing a pistol against the driver's ribs. "Now, we're going to remain completely calm, right?"

The driver raised his trembling hands.

"Nuh-uh. Does a calm man hold his hands up?"

They quickly lowered.

"Good. Now, we're all going to sit here calmly, and wait for the general. If you try to signal anyone, you'll be shot. It's imperative that our mission not be interrupted by whatever trivial matters are going on outside this vehicle, understood?"

"You-you mean this isn't because of you?"

"Of course not. We're all loyal citizens, are we not?"

The man's head bobbed rapidly.

"Good. We're on a mission of the utmost importance, and that timeline cannot be interfered with. This is a prison camp, as you're well aware. The filthy Uyghur Muslims we hold here are always causing trouble. I have no doubt they're to blame for what's occurring right now. Are we all in agreement?"

The driver nodded unconvincingly, the weapon pressed against him apparently causing doubts. "Yes, Colonel."

"Good." Kane motioned to the fridge and Jack grabbed a Coke and a Snickers bar, handing them forward. "Here, eat something. It will calm you down."

"Th-thank you, sir."

The trembling driver tucked into the offerings while Kane and the others continued enjoying their own, nobody saying anything as he monitored the updates coming from Leroux through his earpiece, and watched the feeds from the drones on Jack's phone.

Something always has to go wrong.

Operations Center 2, CIA Headquarters
Langley, Virginia

Leroux squinted. "Is that General Zhang?"

Tong zoomed in on the image, the computer quickly mapping his face and confirming it. "Yup."

"Here we go." Leroux activated his comms. "Arrow, Control. Zhang just left the admin building. He's coming down the steps now."

Kane didn't reply, and Leroux repeated the update. Kane responded in Chinese.

"General Zhang!"

Leroux glanced at Tong, confusion on both their faces as they watched Kane step out of the limo. "What the hell is he doing?"

Urumqi Training Center

Urumqi, China

Kane stepped out of the limo and beckoned the general. "General Zhang! I must speak with you!"

Zhang froze on the steps, staring at him. "What the hell are you doing in my car?"

Kane beckoned him again. "I can explain inside, General, but not in the open. Orders from Beijing."

Zhang stared toward the barracks, leaving little doubt he was torn between his desire to check on his prisoner, and his duty to obey orders from Beijing. A colorful curse was uttered, then he rushed down the final steps, heading toward the limo. "Who the hell are you?"

"Colonel Liu." Kane held out a hand toward the dark interior of the limo and Zhang growled.

"Beijing better have a good reason for this. I'm in the middle of a security issue."

He climbed inside and Kane followed, closing the door behind them and locking it. Jack leaned forward, pressing his gun against the driver's ribs as Fang flicked on the light, her own gun now pressed against the general's stomach.

"Good to see you again, General."

Zhang cursed, scrambling for the door, but Kane waved his own weapon in front of him.

"Here's what's going to happen. We're going to drive through that front gate. Driver, you will stop when challenged, but you will leave your window up and point to the rear. If you say anything, you will be shot, as will the general. General, I will put down the window. If I run into any trouble, you will tell them to let us through. You will tell them your plane is departing early because Beijing moved up your meeting. I will then close the window, and we will leave. If you give them any indication something is wrong, I will shoot you and the driver."

Zhang laughed. "You'll die as well."

Kane motioned toward Fang. "She's already dead, and he and I are expendable. But I suspect the two of you value your lives. So, does everyone know their part?"

The driver stared at Zhang in the rearview mirror and the general growled. "Do as he says. They'll never get out of China anyway."

"Yes, General." The driver put the car in gear and slowly pulled away as Kane leaned back in his seat.

In the next two minutes, we're either dead or free.

Operations Center 2, CIA Headquarters

Langley, Virginia

Leroux pointed at Tong as he watched the limo pull away. "Send the message to Chan. Tell him to have his people standing by."

"Yes, sir."

"And get me the Chief. We're going to need to send some assets in the area if Kane's doing what Chan claims."

Morrison entered the operations center as if on cue. "I just got your message. They're in?"

"They're in and leaving."

Morrison's eye widened. "They have her?"

Leroux beamed. "Yes!"

Morrison shook his head, his hands on his hips. "Unbelievable. You realize we have to reexamine every case we've had over the past five years where we identified someone as being dead because of their DNA?"

Leroux glanced at him, tearing his eyes away from the displays for a split second. "Please tell me that's not *our* job."

Morrison laughed. "Don't worry, your team is still active ops only." He gave Leroux the stink-eye. "Unless you piss me off."

Leroux grunted. "I won't, but Randy might."

Child grinned. "Happy to do my part." He gestured toward the display. "Looks like we're about to see if this works, or goes south in a hurry."

Urumqi Training Center

Urumqi, China

Fang pressed into the corner of the wraparound bench seating, positioned on the same side as the window now rolling down, her weapon pointed at the driver's back. The partition was down and the internal lights turned off, keeping her hidden from those outside.

She hoped.

She was struggling to keep her emotions in check. Until a few minutes ago, she had been dead. It simply hadn't been a *fait accompli*. She had slit her wrists, hoping to die on her own terms, and even if that had failed, she had an appointment with a can of gasoline and a match.

But now, here she was with the man she loved, his partner whose real face she still hadn't seen, and the general who would have her dead.

And perhaps only moments from escape.

Yet so much could still go wrong.

Kane leaned out the window, his arm propped up, making certain the guard could see his rank. "What's going on?"

"I'm not sure, Colonel. Prisoner escape, I think."

Kane frowned, shaking his head. "When are these Muslims going to learn? Just stay put and appreciate what their country and Party have offered them at no expense."

"I agree, sir." The soldier appeared uncomfortable. "I'm afraid I'm going to have to search the vehicle. Standard procedure during these situations."

Kane smiled. "I understand completely, however we're on a tight schedule. General Zhang's meeting in Beijing has been moved up and we must leave now. No delays." The guard was about to protest when Kane cut him off. "General, perhaps you can set your fine soldier's mind at ease."

Kane sat back in his seat and Zhang leaned over him. Jack's weapon was pressed low against the general's back, reminding the man not to be foolish.

"Let us through, Lieutenant."

The man's eyes bulged and he snapped to attention. "Yes, General!"

Kane pressed the button and the window rose as the guard yelled for the gate to be opened. The driver pressed on the gas, easing the car through the gates. "Turn left and gently pull away."

The driver said nothing, but complied, and Jack held up the phone, an overhead shot of the gate showing it closing with no further action taken by the guards.

"You're going to pay for this. All of you." Zhang glared at Fang. "Especially you." Zhang turned his wrath on Kane then Jack. "And you two. Betraying your country, your people? I'm disgusted with every one of you."

Kane shrugged. "Night-night." He pistol-whipped the man, knocking him out cold.

Fang visibly relaxed, her shoulders slumping. "Now what?"

Kane grinned. "Would you believe I have no idea?"

Her eyes widened. "Excuse me?"

"The next twenty-four hours are a mystery, but I've been assured we're in good hands."

Fang tensed. "Why do I have a bad feeling about this?"

Kane laughed. "Babe, I have no clue what's happening over the next twenty-four hours, but I can guarantee you this: they're nothing compared to the twenty-four after that."

Operations Center 2, CIA Headquarters

Langley, Virginia

Child whistled. "Man, he's got a golden horseshoe up his ass. I've never known anyone so lucky."

Morrison glanced at the young analyst. "Son, if you knew half of what I know about that man, you'd realize he's gone through more hardship and pain than anyone I know, and wouldn't hesitate to give that horseshoe, if he had it, to anyone in this room before using it for himself."

Child flushed. "I'm sorry, sir, I didn't mean—"

Morrison cut him off with a wave of his hand. "Don't worry about it, son. I understand the sentiment." He pointed at the display showing the limo driving away from the concentration camp. "What you just saw here today may look like luck, but it wasn't. That was years of experience, and the reactions and abilities of the best-damned operative I have under my command at work. Remember, he picked the gear that Chan would have in place when they arrived in Beijing. He picked the gear Chan would have in Urumqi when they arrived. Microdrones, uniforms and papers, face masks. It was all his plan. His foresight, then his balls, got him through that gate, into Fang's cell, and into that limo."

"But the limo, we didn't know it was going to the compound. How could he base his entire escape on it being there?"

"I doubt he did, but he's trained to think on the fly. As soon as we told him about the flight, he knew from the briefing notes we sent him that the general always drove by limousine, and that it was always kept at the airport in case Party officials arrived. Zhang didn't mind waiting for the car to come to him, but he would never keep someone who might help him in his career waiting for it."

Leroux turned to Morrison. "So, you think he's trying to advance in the Party?"

"We know he is. He's one of their highest ranked generals, and certainly one of their most feared. He's ruthless, and unafraid to take bold action. Just look at what he's doing with those camps. He has over half a million children behind those walls already. He has scores of these facilities all over western China. He intends to wipe the Uyghur culture and the Muslim religion from China, and with no one challenging him, he'll succeed. People forget the Chinese think long term. He has a generational plan. In twenty-five years, he'll have succeeded if no one stops him. And as their economy continues to grow, so does their military, and so does their middle class. Very soon, they'll overtake us as the largest economy in the world, and then they will decide what happens, not us.

"You can already see it in Hollywood. How many movies now have the Chinese as the heroes? How many movies are now set in China? Their movie-going audience is huge and growing rapidly, while ours is dwindling. While I have no problem with diversity in film, this is different. Studios are forced to imply that China is benevolent and always there to help." He pointed at the screen, the limo making a righthand turn. "That facility is all the proof I need to know they are anything but, and the world needs to wake up and realize that before it's too late."

Leroux cleared his throat, hesitant to interrupt a rare public rant from his boss. "Sorry, sir, but they're about to reach the transfer point."

Morrison held up a hand. "Sorry about that, people, I just got out of a briefing where I heard some shit you wouldn't believe. It has me in a mood."

Child grinned. "No worries, sir, feel free to vent at us any time. It's better than having to listen to Sonya go off on Game of Thrones yet again."

Tong threw her hands up. "Well what do you expect? I spent eight damned years, and—"

Child plugged his ears. "Spoiler alert!"

Leroux stepped toward the display. "Uh oh."

Urumqi, China

Jack cursed and Kane turned to him. "What?"

Jack held up the phone showing the main gate, and both Kane and Fang cursed. The gates were open, and a dozen vehicles were racing through.

All turning in the direction they had just left.

Kane checked his own phone and pointed at an alleyway ahead. "In there."

The driver complied.

"Stop at the red light." Kane gestured toward the unconscious general. "What do you want to do with him?"

Fang stared at Zhang. "He won't stop. He told me too much when he was sure I was going to die. And now he knows how to find us."

Kane put two bullets in the back of the slouched man's skull and the driver screamed. "Shut up or you'll be joining him." The poor bastard, innocent in all this, snapped his mouth shut as Kane shoved the general's body into the far corner of the limo.

Jack wiped some brain matter off his hand. "Warn me next time, would you?"

Kane eyed him. "Have you not been paying attention these past couple of days?"

Jack frowned. "You got me there."

The driver came to a stop beside a red light on the driver's side, and a door underneath it opened, a man stepping out. Kane rolled down the window. "I have three to transport, one to dispose of, and one to keep on ice until we're clear."

The man motioned for them to follow him. He shouted some orders and another man rushed out and yanked the driver out of his seat, taking over his position behind the wheel. A wide garage door opened and the new driver gunned the engine, cranking the wheel as he spun the long vehicle in the tight space, expertly guiding it through, the metal door dropping behind it as everyone stepped inside.

Within moments, there was no evidence they had ever been outside, and any search parties would never find the limo until their new handlers wanted it found.

"What's the plan?" asked Kane.

"You don't need to know," replied a man emerging from the shadows. "Our job is to get you to your destination safely, then hand you over."

"Have you done this a lot?" asked Fang.

"Yes."

"And how many times has it worked?"

"Every time." The man eyed her. "Unless someone doesn't follow instructions, or does something stupid. Are you people who will follow instructions?"

They all nodded.

"Are you stupid people?"

They all nodded.

The man eyed them. "I don't like funny people either."

Jack grunted, jerking a thumb at Kane. "Then you're going to love him."

"No time for this." The man pointed to a room nearby. "In there. Change your clothes, remove anything metal, anything that could be tracked or detected in a scan, then put on the clothes that are there. Wash yourselves, straighten your hair, everything. You cannot look like you just escaped prison."

Fang held up her wrists. "I need to change these bandages."

The man frowned. "I'm not going to ask what kind of coward—"

Kane took a step forward. "Be very careful what you say next."

The man eyed him. "Do you think you intimidate me? If I'm caught, I'm dead."

"I know you don't fear death, but if you screw this up, or piss me off, I'll make sure you never get a contract again. You might not mind dying, but I have a feeling you'd hate being poor again."

The man growled. "I'll bring a medkit."

Kane led the way into the room, quickly clearing it before indicating the others should join him. As he closed the door, he saw the driver being bound and gagged then placed in a chair.

"They seem friendly," said Jack.

Fang agreed. "Lovely people."

Kane chuckled. "Well, remember, they're criminals. For the moment, they're on our side, but that could change in a heartbeat, especially if they find out what's really going on. Let's just play nice, and hope they don't switch sides before we get to our destination."

"Which is?"

"East."

Fang eyeballed him. "You're going to have to explain that."

Harris Residence, Lake in the Pines Apartments
Fayetteville, North Carolina

"Your pan is wobbly."

Command Sergeant Major Burt "Big Dog" Dawson inwardly cringed as Vanessa Moore demonstrated her discovery to his fiancée, Maggie Harris, and several of the other gathered wives and girlfriends of Bravo Team. The apartment was jammed with his comrades in arms, all members of 1st Special Forces Operational Detachment–Delta, commonly known to the public as the Delta Force. He and Maggie were hosting a barbecue, the grill heating up on the balcony while Vanessa, a professional chef, was about to prepare a custom barbecue sauce she swore would bitch-slap their taste buds with every bite.

"BD! You put the pan straight into the sink again, didn't you?"

He grinned sheepishly at Maggie. "Sorry, babe, it's hard to break over ten years of bad habits."

She jabbed a finger into his chest. "You're buying a new one this time."

Vanessa shook her head. "Oh, don't buy a new pan. I can fix it for you. Gotta hammer?"

Her boyfriend, Sergeant Leon "Atlas" James' booming voice cut through the chatter. "I'll do that, babe." He turned to Dawson. "Where's your hammer?"

Sergeant Carl "Niner" Sung took a seat at the breakfast bar. "This should be good." He flexed his pecs. "Hulk smash!"

The impossibly muscled Atlas took the hammer and pointed it at Niner. "That's enough from the pipsqueak gallery."

Vanessa placed the pan upside down on a cutting board, covering it with a dishtowel. "You're sure you can do this?"

"Babe, I've used a hammer before."

He raised it high, and everyone, Delta Operators and better halves alike, winced.

Then he dropped it.

Hard.

"Gently!" cried Vanessa, shoving him aside and yanking away the cloth—revealing an inverse concave pan with the outline of the hammer's face in the center.

"Good job, genius," snorted Niner.

Atlas was aghast. "I don't know what went wrong. I've watched you do it and this never happened."

Vanessa took the hammer from him. "You've got a hundred pounds of muscle on me."

"Only if he's using his elbows."

The women groaned at Niner's remark, but Atlas gave him a behind-the-back fist bump.

"I can fix it. I'll just hit it the other way."

Vanessa shook her head. "No, you'll break the coating. It's ruined now." She turned to Maggie. "I'm so sorry. My boyfriend, whose biceps are clearly bigger than his brains, will be buying you a new frying pan."

Maggie laughed. "Don't worry about it. As far as I was concerned, it was already ruined."

Dawson shrugged. "I've used warped frying pans for years, never bothered me."

Sergeant Will "Spock" Lightman cocked an eyebrow. "Have you ever tasted your cooking?"

Niner grunted. "I have, and there's no way you can blame a warped pan for that."

Dawson stared at them. "Hey! When did I become the target? I thought we were all mad at Atlas!"

Atlas grinned. "I'm too cuddly to stay mad at."

Vanessa snuggled under his arm. "Yes, you are."

Niner leaped over the counter and snuggled under the other. "You're telling me."

Atlas batted him away with a meaty hand, Dawson catching him from crashing into the kitchen island.

Maggie pointed to the living area. "Okay, you boys have lost your kitchen privileges."

Niner punched Atlas as they left. "See what you did?"

"I didn't do it. You're the one who was all touchy-feely."

"So sue me for showing my friend some lovin'."

"If I want lovin', I'll be getting it from Vanessa."

"Can I watch?"

Atlas laughed. "You'd be ruined for life."

Dawson snorted as he fished his vibrating phone from his pocket. "Hello?"

"Mr. White, you're needed."

"On my way."

He ended the call and held up a hand, silencing everyone. "Sorry, folks, I've been called in." He pointed at his team. "Easy on the beers. I have a funny feeling at least some of us are going to be busy soon."

The Underground Railroad

China

Kane lay flat on his back as he had for untold hours with Fang to his right and Jack to hers. It was a special hidden compartment underneath a shipping palette, cleverly disguised so that the outside observer would have no idea it was there.

And it wasn't designed for large American frames.

Kane had little doubt the average slim Chinese citizen escaping the authorities might fit with ease—Fang certainly appeared comfortable—however Caucasians with barrel chests and wide shoulders?

Nope.

Add to that the hunger and thirst, and everything was just peachy.

They had been fed a small meal that he and Fang agreed had turned, though Jack had disputed that and devoured his to the last morsel. Then each was given a single bottle of water.

"Is this enough?"

"Enough to live. Do you really want to be peeing inside there?"

"So, we're in this the entire way?"

"Yes. You're standard cargo, being shipped from a textile factory here to Shenyang. When you arrive at the other end, our people will retrieve you. Whatever you do, don't try to get out yourselves. You could be sitting in an inspection facility."

Kane had rolled his eyes. "If we're in an inspection facility, I'd say we're screwed. If they have dogs, they'll sniff us out in a heartbeat."

The man shook his head. "The entire thing has ground coffee in the inner lining. It throws the dogs off your scent. It's okay, you'll be fine."

And they had been so far, though Kane's entire body ached from his daylong confinement.

"Remind me when we get back to update my will. I want to be cremated. I can't spend eternity like this," whispered Jack.

Kane chuckled. "Me neither. If we have to make a run for it at the other end, I'm screwed."

"I'm feeling pretty good actually." Kane heard Fang roll to her side to face him.

"What I would kill to be tiny like you."

Fang patted his chest. "They're not used to shipping big American boys like you, I guess."

Jack agreed. "Kind of like when you order a large shirt that's made in China, and you kinda wonder if you ordered from the children's section by mistake."

Kane shifted slightly. "I had something similar happen to me in Vietnam. I had to make a quick exit, and had nothing but my birthday suit on—"

"Birthday suit?" asked Fang.

"Yeah, I was naked, like I was on my *birth* day."

Fang giggled. "I love American sayings. Wait. Why were you naked on a mission?"

"I was between missions."

"Oh. Hey!"

"Looong before I met you, babe. So, I'm running from an angry husband—she lied, I swear—and I duck into a tourist shop. All I could find was a G-string swimsuit bottom and a shirt so small it could have been used in an under-boob photo shoot. Try hailing a cab in Hanoi wearing that."

Jack snorted. "I'd have paid to see that."

"Most would have paid not to."

Jack growled. "Oh, God, I'm going nuts over here. I've got an itch I can't reach."

"Let me help," said Fang, flipping around.

Kane reached over and jabbed Jack. "It better not be your nuts."

"No worries, it's my left shin. It's been driving me crazy." Jack groaned in ecstasy. "That feels sooo good."

"That *really* better not be your nuts."

"That's good, Fang, thanks, I think you've got it. Better stop before your boyfriend starts a fistfight in here."

Fang flipped back around to face Kane. "Anything you need scratched?"

Kane grinned in the dark. "Well, now that you mention it."

Operations Center 2, CIA Headquarters

Langley, Virginia

Tong shook her head in disbelief. "The western half of that country is going apeshit. They've sealed the northern, southern, and western borders, grounded all flights in the area, and are searching every car and train leaving the region. I've never seen anything like that before."

Leroux agreed. "Neither have I." He pointed at the display indicating the intelligence reports that were rolling in. "Notice how they're focusing on the shortest routes out of the country? None of them are toward the east. Kane must have realized what they'd do, so went in the least likely direction they would suspect."

Child shook his head. "Smart."

Leroux had some fun with him. "Not just lucky?"

Child groaned. "Yeah, yeah, I know. Am I ever going to live that one down?"

"Probably, but I've got a long time before retirement," said Tong. She gestured toward the displays. "But I *will* give you insane. His evac plan is nuts, and I've seen some of his stunts before. This is crazy even for him. You never go there on purpose."

Leroux folded his arms, leaning back in his chair as the display indicated Bravo Team had just been inserted into the Seventh Fleet. "Which is exactly why this could succeed brilliantly."

Child spun in his chair. "Or fail spectacularly."

USS Comstock

Yellow Sea

Command Sergeant Major Dawson followed the Command Master Chief of the USS Comstock to the wardroom reserved for them while they awaited their final orders to deploy. He heard a bang behind him and turned to see Sergeant Gerry "Jimmy Olsen" Hudson rubbing his head.

"Sonofabitch!"

Niner glanced at him. "You've got quite the bump forming there." He raised his voice. "Hey, anybody got a hammer?"

Dawson chuckled. "Atlas can take a look at that for you if you want."

"It would be my pleasure," boomed Atlas.

Jimmy glanced over his shoulder at the massive man. "Thanks, but I think I'll pass."

"Probably a good idea. What works on frying pans doesn't necessarily work on skulls. Even one as thick as yours."

"Haw-haw."

They stepped inside the wardroom and everyone claimed a chair. The Command Master Chief showed them the amenities then left, closing the door behind him.

Niner voiced what so many were thinking. "So, does anyone else think Kane's plan is FUBAR before we even get out of the gate?"

Dawson shook his head. "I think he's a little nutty, but we've done this before. And *he's* done this before too. Remember those scientists and their families a few years back? But we do have to be careful. The Rules of Engagement on this one are shit. The Pentagon thinks we might escalate tensions not only on the peninsula if we're caught, but with China if we're caught with Lee Fang. At the moment, Washington believes the Chinese have no proof we're behind it."

Spock cocked an eyebrow. "You honestly think they don't know?"

"Oh, they know. Who the hell else would extract her? But without proof, all they can do is assume we're involved. And you know the Chinese, they never like to lose face. They'll never admit we beat their security. They'd rather forget it ever happened."

Niner frowned. "Well, they haven't beaten the Chinese security yet."

The Underground Railroad

China

Jack groaned. "We haven't moved in hours. It has to have been twenty-four-hours by now, hasn't it?"

Kane was in equal discomfort. "I don't know. They didn't let me keep my watch, but I think you're right. All that jostling earlier certainly suggested we were taken off what I'm assuming was a train, then placed somewhere nearby. I'm thinking we're on a loading dock somewhere, and we're supposed to be picked up and taken in a truck to our final destination."

"Yeah, but the question is, are we waiting for Chan's guys to pick us up, or FedEx? If it's our guys, then why would they wait so long? I would have thought they'd be waiting for the train to arrive so they could collect the container right away."

Kane had to agree. "So would I, but with them refusing to tell us how this worked, we're in the dark. Guys like these prefer their routes kept secret, and usually don't like to share."

"Yeah, well, I don't know how much longer we should be waiting before we try to get out of here."

Fang spoke up. "Remember what they said. Don't try to get out on our own."

Jack shifted, stimulating some circulation. "Yeah, I remember, but something's clearly gone wrong. I mean—"

Something pounded against the container and they all fell silent, not willing to risk their whispered conversation being overheard. The sound of a machine echoed through the confined space, and a moment later they were lifted into the air, the jostling ending a few minutes later with an unceremonious slam to the ground. Another few seconds, and a revving truck engine had a wave of relief flowing through Kane.

He squeezed Fang's hand. "Looks like we're going to be okay."

Jack continued to be the pessimist. "Or they're taking us to a police station."

Kane stared at Jack in the dark. "You know, you can be really negative sometimes."

"You know, you're not the first to say that. I blame a misspent youth. What's your excuse?"

"At the moment, too much time with you and those overactive bowels of yours."

"Huh. You noticed that?"

"Hey, those air biscuits you've been launching oh so secretly over the past twenty-four hours haven't exactly been subtle. We told you not to eat that food."

Jack giggled like a little boy. "I was going to blame Fang until I realized she's the only one who can move around in here, so could kill me."

Fang punched Jack and a ripper escaped.

Kane gagged. "Oh, God, dude, stick a cork in it."

"I would ask your girlfriend to do just that if I had one, but that's what she gets for hitting me."

The truck came to a stop and the engine turned off, ending the conversation. A power drill fired up and Fang squeezed Kane's hand. They all remained silent as each of the twelve screws were removed, a number Kane had counted when they were initially sealed inside. Then a sliver of light shone through, then a flood as the section of the container at their feet was removed.

"Oh my God, did someone drop a deuce in there?"

Kane sighed in relief at Chan's voice. Chan grabbed him by the feet and hauled him out and onto the floor. Fang scrambled out after him while he simply lay in place, his eyes adjusting, his entire body one big cramp. Fang and Chan hauled Jack out, who did the same.

"Oh, thank God for fresh air," gasped Jack.

"This is China. There's no such thing." Chan stared at the two men still crumpled on the ground. "So, who's Mr. Farty McFart Face?"

Kane eyed him. "Did you buy that book?"

"I downloaded it. Very interesting. You Americans are weird."

Kane grunted. "You have no idea, my friend." He struggled to an upright position as Fang dropped behind him, massaging his back. "So, what happened? Why were we waiting there so long?"

"Our underground railroad went underground, I think. They never showed up at the rendezvous point, so I paid one of them a visit and got the container number. The rest was easy. We got lucky. If it had sat there any longer, they might have given it a good look. The entire country is looking for you. Good thing you had those masks. Your faces are all over TV."

Kane tensed. "And Fang's?"

Chan shook his head. "No, they're keeping her out of it. I don't think they want to admit she's in the country. You two are wanted for murdering General Zhang. Apparently, you are Uyghur Muslims who were ungrateful for all the good things he was doing for you."

Jack glanced at the others. "That doesn't sound like us."

Chan beckoned them to get up. "Those disguises of yours worked. I have a feeling they have no idea who you are."

"Good." Kane rose with the help of Fang, then hauled Jack to his feet, both of them continuing to stretch, the lithe Fang appearing none the worse for wear. "Does that mean you can't get us to our final destination?"

"No. You were smart coming here. We're nearly at the border already, and nobody is looking here. If you had tried to go any other direction? Forget it."

"Do you have someplace we can clean up?" asked Fang.

Chan shook his head. "No, there's no time. I've got clothes and equipment in the van."

Jack patted his stomach. "Please tell me you've got food and water."

Kane shook his head. "Water only for you. The last thing we need is your stomach finally giving in."

Operations Center 2, CIA Headquarters

Langley, Virginia

Leroux sat at his station, drumming his pencil against his keyboard, a bundle of nerves like the rest of the room. It had been almost 24 hours with no word from Kane, and only a short message from Chan indicating something had gone wrong.

No one had shown up at the rendezvous.

At this point, Kane and the others could be in Chinese custody or worse, and the only thing giving him any hope was that the Chinese appeared to still be on high alert, searching everything leaving the western half of the country. Surely if they had captured them, they'd have called off the search.

Though often the left hand didn't know what the right was doing.

And sometimes it was by design.

A burst of static over the comms had Leroux on his feet, pressing his headset tighter against his ear.

"Control, Arrow. We made it to the exchange point, over."

A round of cheers erupted at Kane's voice, a smile spreading on Leroux's face as he held up a hand to silence the team. "Copy that, Arrow. What's your ETA to the border?"

"One hour. Will our friends be there?"

Leroux snapped his fingers, pointing at Tong. "I'm sending them now. They should be there to rendezvous with you assuming everything goes smooth."

"Copy that. Arrow, out."

He turned to Tong. "Tell Delta they're a go."

Off the coast of North Korea
Yellow Sea

Dawson crouched at the bow of the Zodiac, facing his team. A second Zodiac had just dropped off, waiting outside the twelve-mile limit in international waters as his team was inserted only a few miles from the Chinese border.

"Remember your Rules of Engagement. Do not fire unless fired upon. If everything goes right, no one will ever know we were here. If this turns into a Charlie-Foxtrot, our orders are to fall back. Kane and the others can be captured. Their presence isn't an act of war if they're treated as spies. Ours is. American Special Forces cannot be captured on North Korean territory. Not while that nutbar has nukes. Understood?"

"Yes, Sergeant Major," acknowledged the five others he had selected for the mission. "We're inserting as close to the border as we can, then hoofing it the rest of the way. About five klicks. We'll monitor their crossing, rendezvous with them, then get them out. Quick, quiet, quality work, gentlemen, and we'll be finishing that barbecue in no time."

Atlas groaned. "Why'd you have to mention barbecue? You know I love my barbecue. Now that's all I'm going to be thinking about this entire mission."

Niner cursed. "Great. Let's just turn around now. You know how loud his stomach growls. One hunger pang and the entire northwest of this shithole will know we're here. That thing oughta come with a warning label."

Atlas patted his stomach. "It's okay, boy, he didn't mean it."

"Sixty seconds, Sergeant Major."

Dawson glanced back at the pilot, the Navy crewing the two Zodiacs so they wouldn't be left onshore to be discovered while they collected their people. "Copy that. Check your gear. Sixty seconds."

His stomach growled.

Barbecue would be nice right about now.

Chinese-North Korean Border

China

Unmasked, clothed, fed, hydrated, but still stinking, they had sprinted for several miles after Chan had dropped them off as close to the border as he dared. The good news was that this part of the 880-mile border was porous.

Very porous.

There were few fences and even fewer guards. Each side had a regularly patrolled border road, but the insanity of the Demilitarized Zone separating the technically still at war two Koreas was nowhere to be seen here. China and North Korea were officially friendly, and the only fencing was around cities to minimize North Koreans from fleeing into China.

"Patrol!" hissed Fang as she dropped to her stomach, Kane and Jack following. The headlights of a vehicle were visible ahead, winding along the road, driven far too quickly for anyone to see anything in the dark. These were bored soldiers going through the motions, their orders to complete their rounds in a certain amount of time. He had little doubt they'd stop at some point to kill enough time to make it appear to their commanding officer that they had completed it properly.

The vehicle came to a halt, four men exiting, all taking leaks.

Jack cursed. "You've got to be kidding me. Now what?"

Fang glanced over her shoulder at Kane. "We don't have time to wait for them to leave. Let's assume they're going to be here for too long, and just circle behind them. If we're quiet, they won't hear us, and they've got their headlights on, so their eyes won't pick us out."

Kane agreed with Fang's assessment. "Let's do it."

They scrambled along the rocky hill with the road below, putting distance between them and the patrol, when Jack caught his foot and fell, slamming his knee into a rock. He cried out involuntarily, quickly cutting off the sound, but as Kane turned to help the man, Fang cursed.

"They heard that."

Shouts erupted and the vehicle's engine fired up.

"We've got to hurry."

Jack took a tentative step. "I can barely walk." He cursed. "Leave me. Get her to safety. I'll give them a story."

"Nuts to that." Kane grabbed him and slung him over his shoulders in a fireman's carry, then followed Fang down the embankment and toward the road, the frozen river tantalizingly close. "You go," he said to her. "And no matter what happens, you get across the river. We'll just be a little behind you."

"Nuts to *that!* We all go, or none of us go."

There was no arguing with Fang. Experience had taught him that. Instead, he urged his already screaming legs to work a little harder, and they reached the road with the military SUV less than a hundred yards away, the headlights momentarily highlighting them. Gunfire rang out, tearing at the ground in front of them, and Kane jerked to a halt.

"Put me down," said Jack. "I can't shoot dry humping your neck, and they might not have seen me."

Kane did and Jack scrambled down the slope, hiding behind a rock as he drew his weapon.

"Do we fight?" asked Fang.

"No, we wait. There are too many guns on us. We have to take them by surprise. Jack, you ready?"

"Say the word," came the reply from behind them.

Kane stepped forward, his hands held high, a broad smile on his face as he greeted them in English. "Hi guys! Sorry to startle you. We got lost and I tripped when we were coming down the hill to see you, and boy, are we glad to see you, eh!"

Chinese he understood perfectly was barked at him, but he was in full Canadian mode.

"Sorry about this, like I said, we didn't mean to scare you." He tapped his chest. "Canadian."

One of the soldiers stepped forward. "Canadian? Not American?" He glanced at Fang. "And what about her? She's Chinese!"

Fang smiled. "My parents were. I was born in Vancouver." She wrapped her arm around Kane's. "My boyfriend and I came here to visit my homeland."

"Why are you here?"

"I just said, to visit—"

"No!" The soldier jabbed a finger at the ground. "Why are you *here*?"

Fang laughed. "Oh! Sorry, I misunderstood. We wanted to see the North Korean border. You know, just curious. We hired a guide in Dandong, and when we went hiking, he took off with all our stuff! I thought we were going to freeze to death! Thank God you guys came along!"

Kane took another step forward and a rifle was raised.

"Stay where you are!"

Kane held his hands a little higher, but didn't yield the ground he had gained. "Sorry, sorry. I'm just not used to guns."

His earpiece crackled. "Arrow, Control. We've got another vehicle approaching from the east in an awful hurry. ETA five minutes. Stand by." A moment later Leroux returned in his ear. "We also have three vehicles approaching from the North Korean side. You're going to be knee-deep shortly, over."

Kane squeezed his right hand into a fist twice, signaling his acknowledgment. "Man, I can't wait to get inside your jeep. We're going to be nice and warm in five minutes. Maybe even a little too warm."

The guard's eyes narrowed at Kane's coded message to the others, Kane the only one with comms. "What do you mean?"

Kane pointed at the vehicle. "It's warm in there, isn't it? Can we just sit inside while you sort this out?"

One of the soldiers who had been inside on the radio stepped out, speaking in Chinese. "They said arrest them. We'll sort it out at the station. But be careful, one of them could be who we're looking for."

I guess this gets messy.

Kane stepped forward, crushing the windpipe of the soldier who had been speaking to them with a quick jab of the fist. The man collapsed, grabbing for his throat as he gasped for breath. Fang rushed forward, sweeping the legs out from under the nearest to her before rolling and hammering his neck with a vicious strike while Jack rose to a knee, firing, hitting the third soldier in the shoulder, then the fourth in the outer thigh. Kane surged forward, putting his wounded target into a sleeper hold while Fang executed several roundhouses on hers.

It was over in less than sixty seconds.

Kane pulled some zip ties off one of the soldier's belts, then he and Fang quickly bound the four men. Fang leaned into the vehicle and smashed the radio.

"Do we treat their wounds?"

Kane shook his head. "No time. Their buddies will be here any second. Let's get to that river and across the ice. Once we're in North Korean territory, we'll have an entirely new set of problems to deal with."

Jack grunted as Kane threw him over his shoulder. "Why, what do you know that we don't?"

"I'm not sure you're going to feel better about our situation if I tell you."

North Korean-Chinese Border

North Korea

Dawson watched the action unfold across the frozen river through his scope, smiling in appreciation at the highly effective takedown of the four Chinese border guards.

"He's good," observed Niner as he stared through the scope of his weapon.

Atlas agreed. "He is that. She's damned good too."

Niner grunted. "Not impressed with that Jack guy. Just laid there the entire time."

"He's injured."

"Or lazy. I'm going with lazy. Any guy who can't take the time to come up with a last name isn't really a workaholic in my mind."

Dawson shifted his position, spotting headlights as the second Chinese vehicle rounded the final corner. "We've got company."

"Do we engage?" asked Niner as he shifted his aim.

"Negative. ROEs say we have no involvement until our people cross the border."

"They're on the ice. How the hell do we know when they're across the border? The briefing said the border zigzagged between islands depending upon ethnicity."

Dawson pursed his lips. "It doesn't matter. The Chinese won't cross it. Do you have those custom rounds for your rifle?"

Niner patted his chest. "Yup. Hand made with Russian materials. They'll never know it was us."

"Okay, get ready to use them. We'll put some warning shots in front of them if we have to. I don't want to be killing anyone today unless it's absolutely necessary."

Chinese Border-North Korean

China

Kane sprinted across the ice, the rubber grips and spikes on his boots doing their job, though Fang was having a little more difficulty, Chan not having anything appropriate in her size. He held out his hand.

"Take my hand! I'll drag you, it'll be faster!"

She reached forward and gripped his wrist, then planted her feet, one foot forward, the other at an angle behind her along with her other arm. She glanced behind her. "They're coming!"

Kane risked a quick look then ignored the problem. There was nothing they could do about it. They could engage, but they were extremely close to the border, and if Leroux was right, they would have North Koreans to deal with soon—and the last place he wanted to be was in the middle of a frozen river with no cover, and hostiles on either side. He was putting his faith in his former Bravo Team buddies to be monitoring the situation, though their ROEs forbade them from getting involved at this point.

Gunfire rang out, tearing at the ice to his left, yet he didn't break pace. Every foot he gained was a foot closer to the border and into North Korea where Bravo Team could engage. Another burst of gunfire and Fang cried out, losing her balance. Kane slowed but she scrambled to her feet.

"Are you okay?"

"Go! Go! It's just a flesh wound."

He wasn't so sure because he knew her so well. She'd never risk their lives for her own wellbeing.

Jack added his two cents. "As much as I like my private parts bouncing on your manly muscles, any idea when we might be across this damned thing? From this vantage point, that Chinese shore is looking pretty far away."

Kane shook his head. "No idea, but we're definitely halfway across by now."

More gunfire from behind them was followed by several shots from in front of them.

Kane cursed, his worst fears realized.

North Korean-Chinese Border

North Korea

Niner fired again, putting three more rounds at the feet of the Chinese, then smiled as they tried to hold up on the ice, their feet scrambling under them before they all hit the frozen surface hard.

"Ooh, they're going to be feeling that in the morning."

Atlas chuckled. "A few more rounds and maybe we can open up that ice."

Dawson ended their fun. "They're just soldiers doing their job. As long as they cease fire, then let them be."

Niner continued to observe through his scope. "Well, they're running home to Mommy by the looks of it. And if anyone decides to investigate, they'll blame the Russians, or the ilk they supply."

Dawson rose and headed for the shore. "Niner, Atlas, stand watch. I don't want any surprises."

Kane reached the shore, his lungs burning from the strain and the cold. Fang struggled ashore first when a gloved hand appeared then the grim face of Dawson.

"What the hell have you guys been up to? Trying to start World War Three?"

Fang grabbed his hand and was hauled up and out of sight, then two more hands appeared, Sergeant Eugene "Jagger" Thomas and Spock pulling Kane and Jack onto the embankment and off the ice. Kane flopped on his back beside Jack.

"I'm just...trying to provide...job...security...for you guys."

Dawson stared down at him. "We've got North Korean hostiles about to swarm this area. Planning on a nap or are you waiting for a massage?"

Jack held up a weak finger. "I could use both, please."

Spock cocked an eyebrow. "From what I could see, you were freeloading the entire way."

"It was a choice, and one I stand by."

"He's injured," explained Kane as he was hauled to his feet by Spock. "And so is she."

"It's just a flesh wound," protested Fang as Jagger examined her shoulder.

"BD, we need to treat this, but it can wait."

Dawson headed up the hill. "Good. Grab Jack and let's go. I want to be on those boats in under thirty minutes." He took one last look across the ice to see the Chinese scrambling up the far embankment and toward their vehicle, no doubt about to alert their command to what had just happened.

And then the North Koreans would be alerted, which could mean air and naval assets within minutes.

"Let's move!"

Operations Center 2, CIA Headquarters

Langley, Virginia

Morrison stormed into the operations center, staring at the displays showing an array of satellite, drone, and body camera footage. "Status?"

Leroux, already standing at the center of the room as he managed the op, kept his eyes glued to the action. "They have them and are heading for the evac point, but there's a problem. They incapacitated a Chinese border patrol, but a second group arrived and there was an engagement. Delta followed their ROEs and the Chinese were repelled non-lethally when they crossed the border. But they've called it in."

Morrison cursed. "Any reaction from the North Koreans yet?"

"We already had three vehicles heading toward the area. We think they were listening in on the Chinese broadcast after the initial encounter. They likely didn't know there was anything wrong on their side of the border, but if they don't now, they soon will."

Child pointed at some new intel he had added to the map of the area. "We've got three Shantou-class gunboats heading north, and two helicopters leaving Uiju Airfield."

Morrison cursed again. "Nothing ever goes according to plan. When will our people be at the evac point?"

Leroux shook his head. "Over that terrain, carrying wounded, it could be thirty minutes."

"And when will those ships arrive?"

Child frowned. "About thirty minutes, and the only reason it's taking that long is they don't patrol as heavily at the Chinese border. They always consider the threat to be to the south, so they've got to travel a bit."

"What about those choppers?"

"Ten minutes to the area, then they'll have to search for our people."

Another curse from the Chief. "This is going to get ugly."

Leroux agreed. "Somebody is going to die. Let's just hope it's no one on our side."

North Korean-Chinese Border

North Korea

Kane was on Dawson's tail as they sprinted across the open ground, trying to gain the cover of the trees. Leroux's update had choppers, ships, and ground forces inbound, all of which concerned him to varying degrees. They reached the tree line and Kane smiled as Niner and Atlas greeted them.

"Fancy meeting you guys here."

Niner pulled him up the final few feet. "Well, we heard you got yourself in trouble yet again. We should start issuing bills to the CIA."

Kane grunted as he stretched. "Something tells me your taskmasters already do."

Dawson pointed into the distance. "We've got those three vehicles coming this way. "Niner, you and Atlas spike the road at three points. That should slow them down."

"What about those choppers?" asked Niner.

"One problem at a time. We're heading for the evac point. Spike them then don't look back. We're not waiting for you."

Niner rolled his eyes. "After everything I've done for you?" He jerked a thumb at Atlas. "But let me take Jimmy. This guy's too big to run my speed."

Atlas eyed him. "My problem isn't speed. It's stopping."

"They should have called you Juggernaut."

Dawson pointed at Jimmy. "Go with Niner. Make it fast."

"Copy that." He snapped a two-finger salute then followed Niner, already sprinting in the opposite direction as Dawson turned to Spock. "Take point."

Spock headed out and Dawson addressed the others. "We've got almost five klicks to cover and no time to do it in. Fang, how are you to move?"

"I'm good," she said as Jagger finished wrapping her wound.

"She's good to go," he said. "It'll hold until we get on board."

Dawson pointed at Jack. "Jagger, you take the lazy one. The moment you feel tired, switch off. Nobody plays macho man today. Every second is going to count."

"And when the choppers arrive?" asked Jagger as he grabbed Jack.

"We follow the Rules of Engagement."

Kane frowned. "Which means we wait for them to fire. Lovely."

Operations Center 2, CIA Headquarters
Langley, Virginia

Leroux stared at the display, two helicopters, three gunboats, and three vehicles loaded with who knew how many men, were all converging on their people. He turned to Morrison. "We have to get those ROEs changed!"

Morrison shook his head as he ended his call with Washington. "No go. They're hoping Delta will figure a way out of this without having to engage."

Child pointed at the screen. "That might help."

They all turned and Leroux's eyes narrowed. "What the hell is going on?" One of the choppers was heading the opposite direction, back toward its base. "Were they ordered back?"

Tong offered an alternate explanation. "Well, they're flying buckets from God knows what decade. I'm guessing mechanical failure. They'll probably—yup, there it is. They've deployed a replacement, but he's going to be at least five minutes behind. If our guys can deal with the first one, they might be on the Zodiacs before it arrives."

Leroux sighed. "Only if everything goes perfectly." He turned to the room. "Why do these things never go smoothly?"

Child shrugged. "Because Dr. Seuss didn't write the script?"

North Korean-Chinese Border

North Korea

Niner sprinted through the forest, taking the most direct route toward the road as they could manage through the rough terrain. "Control, One-One. How far out are those vehicles, over?

"You've got three minutes tops, One-One."

Niner cursed. "And how far to the road?"

"We've got you about two-hundred-meters out."

"Copy that." Niner glanced at Jimmy. "This is going to be close." He leaned into it a little harder, then spotted the road ahead, the revving of engines uncomfortably close. He skidded to a halt and dropped to his knees, as did Jimmy, both swinging their packs around and removing a handful of spikes each. They tossed them across the road, making sure they had full coverage.

Headlights highlighted the top of the trees nearby as the lead vehicle crested a rise less than one hundred yards to their left.

"Let's go!" Niner bolted down the road, Jimmy on his heels, making a bend as the lead vehicle hit the spikes. Tires skidding on dirt had a smile on Niner's face as they continued to run. Shouts of anger erupted as he came to a halt, and they scattered a second batch of spikes on the road, repeating the process another couple of hundred yards later. "Control, report."

"All three vehicles have stopped. They're trying to figure out what happened. You've done it, One-One. Now head due west to the evac point. You have three klicks to cover."

"Copy that." Niner got his bearings then pressed forward.

No rest for the wicked.

Kane smiled as the update came through his earpiece. The ground forces had been dealt with, and one chopper was returning to base. Their odds were significantly improving. The thumping of helicopter rotors wiped the smile off his face.

"Does anybody else hear that?" he asked.

"Kinda hard to miss," replied Jack, now over Atlas' shoulder, the muscled warrior just as fast with Jack as the "girly men" were without.

The minutes gained could prove invaluable.

"I can see the shoreline," announced Spock from ahead, still on point. "One klick."

"Copy that!" replied Dawson as everyone pressed on a little harder. They crested the final rise and Kane cursed. The entire terrain was wide open with little to hide behind for when the helicopter arrived.

Someone's going to die.

Niner charged through the brush with his arms crossed in front of him, protecting his face as he listened to the reports from Control and the rest of the team. They were almost at the shoreline, the Zodiacs were inbound, and the chopper's search pattern would have it on-scene shortly.

His friends were hooped.

"Control, One-One. Distance?"

"You're half a klick from the evac."

"And the chopper?"

"Sixty seconds."

"Have the ROEs been suspended?"

"Negative."

What a surprise.

"I need a nest."

There was a pause. "Adjust your heading ten degrees left. Two hundred meters."

"Copy that."

"You'll miss the rendezvous, One-One."

He unslung his weapon. "Yeah, but they won't. One-one, out."

Dawson spotted the first Zodiac hit the shore as the chopper banked into sight, rounding an outcropping to the south. He cursed, then pointed at the boat. "Get the wounded into the Zodiac. The moment they open fire, ROEs say we can defend ourselves. Find whatever cover you can, and prepare to take that mother down."

Atlas rushed toward the Zodiac, weaving between rocks large enough to slow them down, but not enough to provide adequate cover.

Kane pointed after him, looking at Fang. "Go with them!"

She shook her head. "I'm staying. I can't leave them here knowing I'm responsible."

"If you die, then this was all for nothing. Go! If that wound opens up and you start losing too much blood, we might have to carry you out. And remember your wrists. You've already lost too much blood. Go, and don't look back." He grabbed her and kissed her, for what might be the last time. "I love you!"

Tears filled her eyes as the roar of the chopper overwhelmed them. "I love you too!" she shouted as he pushed her toward the Zodiac then took aim at the chopper. It turned to the left, presenting an angle for the door gunner. The muzzle flashed, the roar of a heavy-caliber weapon opening up on them removing any doubt their ROE restrictions had just been lifted.

"Return fire!"

But nobody had waited for Dawson's order, all opening up on the new arrival as Atlas delivered Jack into the waiting Zodiac then grabbed Fang, tossing her inside before pushing the boat off the shore. Its engine gunned and Kane breathed a sigh of relief.

At least she'll survive.

A ship's horn tore through the night, its intense lights casting a glow over the waters, and Kane cursed.

Niner took aim with his rifle, ignoring what was happening to his friends below. It was a distraction from his task. "Taking the shot."

He squeezed the trigger, his aim true, smoke immediately billowing out of the tail rotor. The pilot lost control, and Niner moved onto the next task as he slung his sniper rifle over his back. Jimmy was already prepared, a rope tied to a nearby tree, the other end tossed over the cliff leading to the rocky shore below.

"You know, it's not long enough."

Niner shrugged. "Of course it isn't." With no time to rappel down, he grabbed the rope and swung over the cliff's edge. He let his grip loosen and he slid swiftly down the side of the cliff, staring at the rapidly approaching end of the rope.

He squeezed, killing some speed, then stretched a hand out, grabbing onto a rock protruding from the cliffside, halting his descent with a painful jerk. He looked up to see Jimmy already on his way. Niner pressed against the cliff then let go, squeezing his legs and feet together tight, hoping to avoid another outcropping ten feet below that would tear him open if he hit it.

It whipped past him, scraping up his arm, and he winced before he reached up with his other hand and grabbed it for a split second, killing some of his momentum before his hand slipped and he smacked into the ground hard, rolling to his side.

"It's gonna hurt!" cried Jimmy, not having taken advantage of the natural handholds. Niner rushed toward him, his arms outstretched, and acted as a human catcher's mitt. Jimmy slammed into him, back first, and

Niner let himself fall backward, his backpack helping cushion some of the impact.

But not enough.

He gasped for breath as Jimmy rolled off him, none the worse for wear. He gained his feet and held out a hand for Niner. "You okay?"

Niner took the hand and grimaced as Jimmy hauled him to his feet. "I'll live."

They headed for the shore, the team climbing into the remaining Zodiac as the North Korean ship approached rapidly, the helicopter a smoldering wreck at the far end of the rocky beach. Niner struggled forward and Jimmy urged him onward.

"Hurry! They can't wait!"

Niner growled. "If those bastards leave us after we just saved their skins, I'm swimming after them and tearing them all new assholes!"

Kane dove into the remaining Zodiac as gunfire erupted from the approaching ship, a second visible on the horizon. He grabbed Spock and pulled him inside, then Dawson rolled in last.

"Where's Niner and Jimmy?" he asked.

Spock pointed. "There!"

Kane turned to look as the pilot pulled them away from the shore. He pointed at the man. "Don't you dare leave them!"

"I'm just repositioning!"

Kane gave him a thumbs up and turned back to watch the two stragglers who had just saved all their asses.

"Let's go! Let's go!" shouted Dawson, prompting Niner to flip him the bird.

"What the hell do you think we're doing?"

The man was in obvious pain from something, his face a continuous grimace, and he was slower than usual. Jimmy smacked the side of the Zodiac first, now floating in several feet of water, and hands reached over, yanking him inside, Niner soon flopping on the bottom as well. The pilot gunned the engine, sending them roaring perpendicular to the approaching ship. Gunfire tore into the water ahead of them in an apparent attempt to head off their escape rather than kill them.

That could play to their advantage.

Kane struggled toward the pilot. "Turn toward them!"

The man's eyes went wide. "Are you nuts?"

"Turn toward them, head for their port side, then turn hard to starboard and head straight out to sea."

"It's your funeral."

The pilot banked left and Dawson grabbed Kane by the shoulder. "Care to explain?"

"No time. Just take out their lights! Those old crates don't have anything sophisticated on them. If we can lose them in the dark, it might just buy us the time we need."

Dawson shook his head. "You're crazy, you know that?"

"But you love me!"

Dawson turned to the others. "Take out their lights!"

Everyone took aim, opening up on the rapidly approaching vessel, and Kane just thanked their lucky stars it wasn't a destroyer or worse.

Here's to a shitty navy.

Operations Center 2, CIA Headquarters
Langley, Virginia

Leroux stepped closer to the displays, Morrison joining him. "What the hell are they doing?"

Apparently, he wasn't alone in his shock. "Who turns *toward* the navy *ship* that's shooting at you?" exclaimed Child.

Leroux pointed at the footage streaming in from a drone deployed from the support vessel. "Their lights are going out. And those are muzzle flashes from our guys. They're taking out the lights!"

"What good is that going to do?"

"The North Korean ships can't engage or track something that small and that close. Hell, even we had problems with that. Remember the USS Cole? If they can confuse them long enough, they might just get away."

Morrison frowned. "Only if they don't get killed in the process." He turned to Tong. "Make sure our ship is as close as it can get. I want no more than six inches between their hull and the twelve-mile limit."

"Yes, sir!"

North Korean Territorial Waters

The pilot banked hard to starboard, heading them directly out to sea, the gunfire dwindling behind them as Bravo Team continued to pour lead in the direction of the North Korean ship, keeping the gunners confused. This wasn't a massive vessel they were dealing with, though a properly equipped US vessel of similar size would have shredded them within seconds.

This was a battle between a fifties-era ship and battle-hardened troops.

"ETA?" Kane asked the pilot.

"We've gotta cover eleven miles before they figure out what just happened. We've got about five minutes until we're in international waters."

Kane glanced back at the North Korean vessel as it banked hard to port, its engines fully engaged. "We should be able to outrun that crate in this."

The pilot grunted. "This baby will do fifty-five knots. But it's not the ship I'm worried about, it's her guns!"

The ship's 1.5" gun pounded the air, a shell exploding about fifty feet off their starboard side. Kane joined the others as another shell thundered from its turret, exploding on the opposite side.

"I don't think they're bothering with warning shots anymore," said Jack.

"I don't think they can see us!" yelled Spock from his perch at the rear of the Zodiac. "They're firing randomly!"

Niner frowned. "Well, there may not always be a winner when the wheel spins, but sometimes there is."

Jimmy agreed. "Yeah, well let's hope it's not their lucky day."

Atlas grunted. "Those Commies should know to always bet on black."

Niner eyed him. "Okay, Wesley, how long have you been waiting to say that?"

Atlas shrugged. "About fifty missions, I think."

Another shell threw a wall of water over the boat, momentarily swamping them.

"I think we should have bet on red!" shouted Niner.

Suddenly a blaze of lights filled the night sky ahead of them, a siren sounding and a voice over the PA system broadcasting. "This is the USS Comstock. You are in international waters. Disengage immediately or you will be fired upon." The message repeated in Korean as the Zodiac surged into the back of the dock landing ship, its docking well awash.

Kane caught a glimpse as the North Korean vessel banked hard to port, beating a hasty retreat toward the other two vessels about to enter the fray. He climbed from the Zodiac and Fang rushed toward him, hugging him hard, kissing him harder.

He finally let her go. "Are you okay?"

She patted her freshly bandaged arm. "I'll live."

"And Jack?"

"They're taking him to the infirmary. It's just a twisted ankle and a banged-up knee. He'll be fine." Fang held out a hand toward a wincing Niner. "Are you okay?"

He squirreled up his face, jerking a thumb at Jimmy. "I would have been if this moron hadn't fallen twenty feet onto me."

Kane winced for his friend. "Cracked ribs?"

"Possibly. Hoping for just bruised."

Atlas joined them, slapping Niner on the back, the poor bastard screaming out in pain. Atlas appeared genuinely concerned. "Sorry, you okay?"

"I think I've got *broken* ribs now."

Atlas held out his left arm, pointing at a scratch and a raised bump on his wrist. "I got a booboo too."

Niner eyeballed him from a hunched over position. "Somebody get me a hammer."

Inova Fairfax Hospital

Falls Church, Virginia

Kane walked down the hallway of the hospital holding Fang's hand. He hadn't been able to get the smile off his face since the moment they had boarded the USS Comstock. It had meant they were both safe.

And he still couldn't believe she was alive.

Her homecoming had been a celebration of just holding each other in bed for hours, falling asleep in each other's arms.

Followed by vigorous activity they both equally partook in.

Cleaning up the mess two weeks of drinking and mourning had created.

"Are all men pigs, or just you?"

"I'm going to go with all. I don't come off too good the other way."

Once the apartment had been returned to Fang's exacting standards, the clothes had come off.

And they were promptly interrupted by Leroux's phone call.

Kane knocked gently on the door of Sherrie's hospital room. "Can we come in?"

Sherrie smiled, waving him and Fang inside. "You better! Chris has been telling me what's been going on while I've been having my little nap."

Kane closed the door, everything about to be discussed classified. Fang took Sherrie's hand.

"I'm so sorry this happened to you."

Sherrie gave her a look. "Umm, I don't remember you beating the shit out of me."

Tears rolled down Fang's cheeks. "No, but if they weren't after me, then you never would have been hurt."

Sherrie patted her hand. "Don't worry about it. I'm alive, I'm going to make a full recovery, and I'll be back kicking the asses of America's enemies in no time."

Kane laughed. "I'll warn the world."

"You better." Sherrie sighed, staring at the walls surrounding her. "I can't wait to get out of here. Thank God I was asleep for most of this. Three weeks in here would have driven me nuts." She winked at Leroux then turned to Fang. "Did you know they frown upon you having sex in here?"

Leroux flushed and Kane grinned, extending a fist bump toward his friend.

"Dude, please tell me you tried."

Leroux bumped the fist. "Ahh, no. She's still too weak."

Kane's grin widened. "You stallion, you!"

A nurse entered. "Okay, people, visiting hours are over. I want you all out of here."

Leroux opened his mouth to protest.

"Yeah, yeah, *you* can stay a little longer."

Fang gave Sherrie a gentle hug. "We'll come by tomorrow, then we'll get that lunch we were supposed to have when you're feeling better."

Sherrie gave a thumbs up. "Yeah, and after what just happened, you're buying."

Kane laughed and he and Fang left the room, heading for the elevators.

"Did you hear from Jack?"

"Nope."

"Do you expect to?"

"Only if he wants something."

Fang leaned her head against his arm. "Yeah, I guess we owe him one, don't we?"

Kane smiled, thinking of the hotel room in Macao. "You have no idea." His eyebrows rose. "Speaking of owing someone, I just remembered I owe someone a box of steaks!"

THE END

ACKNOWLEDGMENTS

As some of you might already know from following me over the years, I have always wanted to be a writer. I wrote my first "novel" when I was five years old. It was a school project, and I had to write a story, illustrate it, then fold the pages in half and bind it into a little book.

I still have it to this day.

It was a fairy tale about a prince and princess who get married, though unlike most fairy tales, this one didn't have a happy ending—everyone died in the end. I even have blood spilled on the floor in my illustrations. I have a feeling I traumatized some people with it, and it's probably why I don't write children's books.

I wrote short stories for years, many for school, many for myself. When I was twelve, I had my first non-fiction articles published in some of the leading computer magazines at the time (for the nerds, those were Compute!'s Gazette and Run! Magazine). I wrote those for several years, then when I went to university, it all stopped. For years, the only things I read were technical manuals. I rediscovered my love of reading by accident, then after nearly a decade of a vision of a young girl walking through tall grass, the blades flowing between her fingers, I wrote my first short story as an adult.

Then shelved it.

A few years later, I mentioned it to a friend of mine, and she insisted I let her read it. I did, and she loved it. She encouraged me to get it published, so I tried, and it was accepted by a small literary journal. Several short stories later, and The Protocol was written then published.

Fifty books later, and my life has completely changed.

And much of that is thanks to the woman who encouraged me.

Michèle Easey.

My eternal thanks once again go out to her.

On another note, the woman mentioned in the preface, the CIA's Disguise Chief, Jonna Mendez, has a surname that might sound familiar in context. Her late husband, Antonio "Tony" Mendez, was the CIA agent that inspired the movie Argo, and was played by Ben Affleck.

And on yet another note, some might be questioning the DNA science presented in this book. I know I would! The real Chris Leroux sent me the New York Times article talking about it. I'm certain a quick Google search will put you on the right track.

As usual, there are people to thank. My dad for the research, Greg "Chief" Michael for some US Navy info, the proofing team, and of course my wife, daughter, mother, and friends. Also, some honorable mentions from my various Facebook Character Naming Contests: Robert Meaney, Wendy Hartling, and Graciela Estigarribia. Follow me on Facebook at https://www.facebook.com/jrobertkennedy/ to participate.

To those who have not already done so, please visit my website at www.jrobertkennedy.com then sign up for the Insider's Club to be notified of new book releases. Your email address will never be shared or sold, and you'll only receive the occasional email from me, as I don't have time to spam you!

Thank you once again for reading.

Printed in the USA
CPSIA information can be obtained
at www.ICGtesting.com
LVHW041254151023
761121LV00001BB/118